My Montana Ride

My Montana Ride

LB Cotton

Mini Matti Books

My Montana Ride

By LB Cotton

First published in 2021 by Mini Matti Books.
info@minimatti.com

Front and back cover by Janet Thatcher, Ligerwolve Designs
www.ligerwolvedesigns.com

Edit by Fadwa Baraba

American English is the editing language

ISBN 978-1-7398665-0-1 Paperback
ISBN 978-1-7398665-1-8 eBook

To anyone who dare to live their dream.

Acknowledgement

I would love to thank all who have been part of this journey with me. I am so pleased with what has come out of it and I can't thank you enough for all the help, support and encouragement you all have given me over the last two years.

When I joined an *Inspire* group back in January 2020 run by Colin Egglesfield, I had no idea what journey it would take me on. I met a lot of new people from around the world who have become my support team in this journey.

A special thanks to Colin Egglesfield for pushing me to start writing. Janet Thatcher for the lovely cover design and all your encouraging messages. Fadwa Baraba for the editing and for putting up all the changes I kept doing. Heather and Kerri for listening to me.

Last but not least my family for your love and support.

{ 1 }

The light breeze made gentle waves on the long grass as they rode across the plain. The air was clear and in the distance was the majestic mountains. So peaceful. The birds singing and the sun shining from a blue sky. Yes, there is a reason why they call it "Big Sky" country.

A perfect day as far as Ben was concerned.

He was leading a group of tourists on a trail ride, which would take them up on to the small plateau south of the ranch then across the plain and down the other side through a small forest, along a river and then back up again and home. A round trip of about two hours. On the top of the plateau looking west you can clearly see the mountain range in the distance. Ben could never get tired of looking at them. There was something magical about them, a bit like a solid focus point in the distance.

People often made the comment that it was a beautiful part of the world he lived in. Ben couldn't really comment on it as he had lived here all his life and therefore didn't know anything different. He was the third generation on the Jackson Ranch and his hope was that one day there would be a fourth.

Ben's thinking got interrupted by yet another question from one of the participants - one of many from the same one. *Not another one*, he thought.

The questions could be anything from wild life, farming to personal – the last one being the ones that Ben didn't like to answer. He couldn't really see why he should tell them about his personal life.

"Why has a handsome and good-looking cowboy like you not got a wife or girlfriend?"

"Who says that there isn't one?" He hoped that would be enough. Occasionally, he lied, especially if it was young ladies asking. He had learned over the years that that was the best answer to that question and that way they wouldn't ask for his number when they got back.

Finally, they had reached the edge of the plain where you start to ride down towards the yard. From here you could see the main part of the ranch, the house, the barns and the yard. It had been a long day and Ben couldn't wait to get back. The letter was still fresh in his mind; he had no idea what it was but it looked important. It could have been from the Bank and it had given him a feeling of not being good news. His parents hadn't said anything at lunch and Ben decided that if they didn't mention it this evening, he would. For now, he had to stop thinking about it and concentrate on getting this group of riders home.

It was time for some practical information but not before Ben had brought the group to a halt and pointed out the area that they farmed. Somehow seeing it made it much more real for people and made them realize the actual size of the place. He then finished off with the practical information about what to do when they got back to the yard.

"I'd like to thank you all for joining us on this ride today.

Hope you enjoyed it and we'd love to see you back again. For those of you who haven't paid yet, please make sure you see Emma before taking off. Thank you."

Emma had seen them heading down towards the yard and was ready to help once they were back. Most of the riders could get off on their own, sometimes one or two needed a little help. For safety reasons everyone had been told to hold on to their horse until either Ben or Emma was ready to take over.

Ben was lucky to have Emma helping him. She was a natural when it came to handling customers, much better than him. Each rider had to sign a piece of paper to say they understood what the risk was with riding out and that job was Emma's along with making sure that every participant had paid. On top of that, she was also a natural when it came to handling horses and dealing with the cattle and there was something about her that made Ben feel better when he was with her. She was always so happy; in fact, he couldn't remember ever seeing her not happy. She liked things being kept tidy; nothing was left out of place when she was around. Ben was a bit the same. His grandfather had taught him that if you put things back where they should be you could always find it when you needed it.

It didn't take them long to get the horses sorted and turned out. Emma dealt with a couple that had to pay – normally she preferred that everyone had paid before the rides but occasionally, some did afterwards. Soon it was just the two of them left to put saddles away, lock up and head back to the main house.

Ben was looking forward to get in and switch off. The day just felt like going on forever and ever. It wasn't that he didn't enjoy these rides but his mind was otherwise occupied today. It had been one of those "lots of questions" type of day that seemed to go on forever; he had tried his best to be polite and answer them all.

As they were finishing up, Ben's thoughts returned to the letter which he was pretty sure was from the Bank. This spring had been quieter than normal in terms of rides. Ben started to think of what he would do if they had to sell the ranch. He had grown up with it, never worked anywhere else and when his father couldn't do it any longer it seemed logic that he took over. The guilt started to build; he couldn't and wouldn't let his parents down. This was still their business after all. Admittedly there were probably things that could do with being brought up to date. The number of bookings had been falling but *as long as there is still money coming in, it is good enough for us* – they kept saying. There had been a ride today but it wasn't every day that that happened now. Ben wasn't sure why the spring had been so quiet as they hadn't done anything different from last year and the weather had been fine.

Ben had tried to bring up the subject a couple of times but his father's answer every time was: "No need to change, it's just a quiet year."

His mother never said anything in these discussions and if Ben asked her, she would only say: "You heard your father."

He had to face the fact that they weren't prepared to

make changes and it would be down to him to try and find a way through this.

He thought of John, his older brother, who had decided soon after school that he was definitely not going into the ranch life. Growing up, Ben and John were not alike at all. John was a good rider and had taken part when he was needed but he preferred books and numbers. Ben on the other hand loved the great outdoors and the horses.

He was beginning to think if there was a better option or different lifestyle out there for him and if so, what would it be? John seemed to be doing well in whatever business he was working in; Ben couldn't remember exactly what it was but it had something to do with banking. His brother always sounded so happy when they on a rare occasion spoke to him. It had been a long time since Ben last spoke to his brother and the visits didn't happen too often either. As a matter of fact, he couldn't even remember when his brother had last been home. Their parents, who had lived here all their life had never understood why John decided to move right across the country to New York and not follow the family tradition. It had hurt them and they rarely mentioned him in conversations.

When people asked about John, Helen, their mother, just said: "He is a very busy man."

Ben knew it was her way of dealing with it. Bill, their father, was bitter about it and never really mentions John.

A few years ago, Ben had gone to New York to visit his brother and he discovered that big cities weren't his thing. No, he was much happier here in the great outdoors. He couldn't understand how anyone could live in a city. The noise – even at night, the buzzing of the place and the smell of traffic, always someone next to you. And you couldn't see the stars at night. No, city life was definitely not for him; that, he was pretty sure of.

"I think that's all done for another day," Emma came out from the tack room. "Just need to get the cash box and paperwork and I am ready to head back to the house."

She looked at Ben who managed to mutter a thank you.

After making sure everything was locked up and secure, they headed back in silence. Emma stopped just before they got to the back door, grabbed his arm and looked at him.

"It's going to be okay," she was looking straight at him, he had nowhere to escape to however hard he tried to avoid eye contact. "We'll get through this. I know we will."

What - where did that come from? Why would she say that? And "we", what did she mean by that? Ben was so taken aback by her words that he didn't know what to say. *Was it really that obvious?* All he could mutter was: "Okay."

He had to admit that Emma was probably the person who knew and could read him best. What would he do without her? She was a year younger than him and had been coming on the ranch since she was a schoolgirl. She loved the horses but as her family lived in town there was no way she could have her own so Helen and Bill had let her help out as much as she could or would. That had led to her now working for them. Bill had been very impressed with her way of handling horses and had said that she had a very natural way with animals. He had taught her along with Ben and John some of the skills of being a cowboy.

Occasionally some of the customers thought she was Ben's little sister. In fact, Ben himself sometimes had to remind himself that she wasn't. His mother on the other hand did treat her like the daughter she never had, especially after John moved away.

As they walked in through the door, they were greeted by a lovely smell coming from the kitchen, almost the first room you got to as you came in through the back door. Helen was busy cooking.

"Dinner will be ready soon!"

"Thanks, mom." Ben headed in across the hallway and into the living room where his father was sat looking at something. Emma headed to the office at the back of the house to put the paperwork and the money box away.

"Would you like to stay for dinner?" Helen looked at Emma.

"No, thank you, not today. It's dad's birthday and I promised I'd have dinner with them tonight," she went in to find Ben to let him know that she would be back in the morning.

"See you tomorrow," said Helen.

Emma headed for the door. Just before leaving she put her head around the door to the kitchen and said, "Oh, there's some cash in the box. If you get it ready, I could take it to the bank tomorrow unless you or Bill are going into town."

"Thanks, Emma. I'll have a look at it and probably send

Bill in tomorrow. Say hi to your parents and wish your father a happy birthday from us."

For once Ben was glad that Emma wasn't staying. He wasn't in the mood for happy talking over dinner tonight. There were too many things on his mind and in fact, if dinner could be done quickly so he could retire to his place, that would be ideal. Emma's comment just before they walked into the house had added to the mess in his head.

Not a lot was said at the table; it almost felt like there was a heavy cloud hanging over them. One thing Ben did notice was that his mother wasn't eating a lot. He decided that she maybe just wasn't hungry. Then – almost out of nowhere he found himself asking about the letter and immediately regretted it. *Too late now.*

Bill put down his knife and fork quickly and sharply then looked at him.

"What letter?"

"Come on, dad. I saw there was a letter by the diary this morning and I am pretty sure it was from the Bank. Are you gonna tell me what it's about?"

Helen looked nervously at Bill then turned to Ben.

"It's nothing to worry about, Ben."

He didn't believe a word of what she said but before he could say anything Bill started asking about the ride today – like where he had taken them and what horses he had used. *A quick way to changing the subject*, Ben thought and it just made him even more convinced that something bad was up. Knowing how stubborn his father could be, there was no way he was going to get an answer tonight so he dropped the subject and went on to answer his question instead.

It had been very hard for Bill to accept that he had to retire from the physical work, and that his riding days were over. Ben knew that his father really missed taking the rides but age and health issues had caught up with him. It was mainly his hips; they were hurting now and in the end the pain had made the decision for him. Life becomes very hard when you can't do what you love to do. At least he could still drive the truck up and check the cattle and should Ben need anything he could collect it. It was small things but it made him still involved in the daily work.

Back to the questions. Ben couldn't help thinking that they could ask him questions but he wasn't allowed to ask them or he could but wouldn't get an answer. He did his best to try and remember all the things he had talked about on the ride; the horses they had used and also a bit about what he had seen in terms of wildlife.

Once he had finished his report he went on to the subject of the cattle.

"Are the cattle okay for grass?" Ben had asked his father to check them that day as he and Emma had been helping a neighboring rancher move some cattle in the morning.

"Yeah, they can last another week or so before they will need new grassing" was Bill's reply.

Ben made a note to himself that he would have to check where he should put them next and maybe organize some help for it too. Then he turned to his mother and asked,

"Any booking for tomorrow?"

"Only five in the afternoon," she replied.

Was that all? He nearly said it out loud but managed to stop before it came out. Instead, he replied:

"Okay, it will give me time to check out the next field for the cattle."

He got up, it had been a long day and he wanted to hit the bed early tonight.

"See you in the morning," he said and headed out the door and down the drive to his place.

On days like this it was nice to be able to escape to his own place. He needed to get his head straight. Emma's remark still puzzled him along with his mother's reaction to him asking about the letter. Also, it hadn't been the most joyful ride today either. The best part of the day had been helping with the cattle move that morning. One thing Ben would never get tired of was working together with his horse on those kinds of jobs.

As he got in, he went straight to the fridge and grabbed a beer. That was about the only thing he had in the fridge or in the house for that matter. In fact, all he used the house for was sleeping. The rest of the time he would be up at the house or out on the ranch working. It only contained the bare essentials like a couple of chairs and a couch on which he dropped on to and turned on the TV.

He spent some time flicking through the channels, and surprisingly there was really nothing he wanted to watch. In the end, he gave up. The day's event was still running through his head. *Let's hope tomorrow will be better* he thought to himself as he finished his beer and headed to bed.

A beeping noise from the alarm clock woke him up. It took a little while for him to come round. *What a night it had been.* Ben wasn't sure if it was bad dreams or reality but it hadn't been nice. His thoughts immediately turned to the letter and the way his father had cut him off on the subject. It annoyed him that he hadn't managed to get an answer out of them last night. Maybe he would get a chance to look at it today at some point. Right now, he had to try and put it all to one side and focus on the jobs for the day.

A ride up to the cattle and round the field would do him good. It had been a good season in terms of calves and although it was early, maybe if he had an idea of how many he could sell later it could please the bank.

As Ben walked through his house, he could see up to the main house. Something caught his eyes; was that his father letting the chickens out this morning? The chickens were his mother's pride. She was very protective of them and for as long as he could remember, she was the one dealing with them, a job she wouldn't normally trust anyone else with. On the other hand, he also knew his father hated them, maybe because he was the one that had to do the deeds when one had to go.

Suddenly, Ben remembered that his mother hadn't eaten a lot the night before and wondered if that had anything to do with it.

As he walked into the kitchen he looked closely at his mother.

"Morning, mom. Since when have you started trusting dad with the chickens?"

"Morning, Ben. I'm not feeling so great this morning, think I got a cold coming on and he offered to do them. Now sit down, your breakfast is ready."

Ben did as he was told and as she poured his coffee, he couldn't help feeling that something was wrong. Bill came in with fresh eggs.

"How many do you normally have in the morning? This is all I could find", he gave her the basket with the eggs.

"That's fine, thank you. Now sit for your breakfast." She brought two plates across with toast and scrambled eggs. Nothing was said – it almost felt like no one was allowed to say anything. In the end, Ben broke the silence.

"I am riding up to check the cattle this morning. Will try and have a guess on how many we can sell later in the season."

"Hmm a bit early to start thinking of that. Don't you think, son?" Bill looked at him.

Ben nearly said that it could maybe help with their bank issue but his father's look told him that this conversation was finished, and he realized that there was no point continuing; they were not going to tell him what was in that letter. No, he would have to read it himself at some point. Instead, he got up, took his plate across to the sink, and looked at his mother. Did she look a bit pale or was it just his head playing games with him?

"Thanks for breakfast. I'll head out now. See you later."

"Okay, son. Enjoy your ride." She gave him a smile.

Once outside he marched up towards the yard kicking a few stones on the way as a way of letting some of his frustration out. At the yard he was met by Emma, who had watched him coming.

"Morning! What's up with you this morning?"

He had completely forgotten to tell her about the plans for the day.

"Sorry, Emma. I should have told you that there isn't anything until this afternoon."

"I know; I had a quick look at the diary last night when I put the paperwork in. The saddles are due for a clean and check-up so I thought I'd do that this morning while I have time as I know this isn't one of your favorite things to do," she laughed.

She was right; he hated the cleaning part. As a child, him and his brother's job was to do the regular saddle cleaning. However, it was an important part of the job not only for safety reasons but it was also important that the horses were comfortable with the saddles. Ben felt a bit bad about leaving Emma to do the cleaning while he was out riding and for a second, he thought of asking her to join him. On the other hand, he felt he needed to be alone right now.

"Good plan. Make sure you are done so we can ride out this afternoon."

"Don't worry, I will have it all done by the time you are back." She gave him a smile.

Just before heading out, he turned to Emma and asked, "Have you noticed anything different with my mother lately?"

"No, why?"

He told her what he had noticed and the fact that his father was doing the chickens this morning.

"She's been quiet lately. Do you think there's something wrong?"

"Not sure but I have a feeling she's hiding something," he nearly said that both of them were but decided not to.

"I'll talk to her and see what I can find out and let you know."

"Thanks, Emma. Okay, I'm out. Will be back before lunch."

He headed up the track around the back of the barns and up to the road going west with the sun behind him. Ben had no intention of rushing this ride which was why he had said before lunch. First, he wanted to check the cattle then have a look at where to move them to and when.

One of the advantages with being on horseback is that you have time to look around at the land as you are going along, looking out for what wildlife there is and also checking the grass or more the amount of it. Ben noticed that the land still looked fairly green; it wouldn't be long before it would be time to cut it for hay. Later in the summer the grass would get thinner and lose the green color as the ground dried up.

He spotted a couple of deer a bit off the road in front of him, they hadn't noticed him. Ben brought his horse to a gentle halt so he could admire them for a little while. He had always thought of them as very elegant animals and would never get tired of watching them. He watched them for a while but then remembered he had jobs to do and carried on up the road.

Finally, he reached the cattle. They were all together not that far into the field. *Perfect*, he thought and started to ride around them. The cattle just continued eating and didn't really take any notice of him or the horse. There were too many to count but he could see that the calves were growing well and if the summer stayed nice, there would be a fair number to sell later. The next question was when to move them. He rode a bit further into the field to have a look at what grass there was. Well enough for now but his father was right; it would probably be best to move them soon.

He headed back out on the road and towards home. The next field for the cattle was on the way home. It would be a simple move which him and Emma could do with a little help from his father. No need to call in help from some of the other ranches this time. He had reached the gate and went in but instead of riding around to check the fence he headed straight for the river which was running along the bottom of the far side of the field.

He got off, tied the horse up to a tree so it was in the shade and went to his spot. Sitting here watching the river had a very relaxing impact on him. Ben had spent many hours fishing from here. The river was very calm this time of the year and a bit further back you could cross it on horseback. One of his longer trail rides would be following the river up from home and crossing over just before his favorite spot here. Maybe they should do that today as he would have Emma with him to pick up the rear end. It would however depend a bit on the type of riders that was in the group. If there were too many that were very scared of riding but still wanted to do it, it wouldn't work.

Emma was waiting for him when he got back. She had finished the cleaning – well, apart from the saddle that was on his horse. She wanted to get that done before lunch.

"So, what have you decided about the cattle?" she asked.

"Moving them on Monday and as they are only going down the road to the river field, I think we'll be okay. You and I can drive them and dad can turn them into the field."

"That would work – we just gotta make sure that Monday morning is free."

Ben thought to himself that the chances of that was pretty good at the moment unfortunately. He wished he knew the reason for the lack of business, but before he had a chance to think more on the subject, Emma wanted to know more.

"Did you check the fence? You were gone for quite a while."

"Oh, no. I somehow ended up down by the river." Ben was hoping she wasn't going to ask why. After all, she knew it was his favorite spot. "I thought that you and I could check it over the weekend. By the way, the river is nice and calm so if the group is okay, I think we will take them up that way this afternoon."

"That's a good idea and sure, I'll help you with the fence."

The afternoon ride did go the river way and turned out to be a really nice group of people where everyone including Ben enjoyed it.

{ 2 }

The day had arrived and Ben was looking forward to the cattle drive, not that it was going to be that big a thing. He loved this part of his job – working together with his partner, the horse was something he would always enjoy. He spotted his father out doing the chickens again as he headed up to the house for breakfast.

"Morning, mom. I see dad is doing your chickens again." He looked at her as he walked into the kitchen. *She doesn't look that well,* he thought but before he could say anything she said,

"Nah, just not feeling that good today, it's nothing to worry about. I'll be fine once I've had breakfast."

He hoped so; what would he do if she became sick? A cup of coffee and his breakfast arrived in front of him. Bill came in and joined him. They had nearly finished when Emma turned up looking very cheerful as always.

"Morning, everyone! How are we all today?"

"Morning, Emma. Do you want some coffee before you head out?" Helen had already poured it in anticipation that she would say yes.

"Yes, please, Helen; that would be great." She went to sit down next to Ben.

Even after all the years of Emma being around the family Ben still felt uncomfortable with her sitting too close to him and yet at the same time, he always hoped she would pick the seat next to him. He quickly finished his coffee and got up.

"Better get going." He thanked his mother for breakfast. "Take it easy this morning, mom. Make sure you get some rest. We can't have you falling sick on us." Then he turned to his father.

"Will call you when we get to the cattle. No need for you to be out there waiting for us."

As he was heading for the door, he looked at Emma who was still drinking her coffee.

"Are you coming?" He couldn't help smiling a bit.

Emma quickly downed the coffee, got up and thanked Helen for it on the way out of the door.

Ben made sure they were well away from the house before he said anything.

"Did you notice anything different with mom this morning?"

"Not really but then I wasn't there that long. Why?"

Ben wasn't sure if he should tell her or not, maybe he had got it all wrong. Probably best if he just forgot about it. Emma could see that something was up. She had become a bit of an expert when it came to Ben and his mind.

"Ben, I'll talk to her at lunch but I am sure she is fine."

Soon they were on their horses and heading out west. Blue sky and with the sun behind them, Ben was busy admiring the mountains when the silence was broken by Emma's voice.

"What would you do if you weren't doing this?" she looked at him. Caught off guard again. Ben had no idea what to say.

"Don't know, why?"

"Just wondering. It'd be pretty difficult to replace this with something else. There are not many jobs where you have a view like this," she looked at him and smiled.

He fully agreed with her on that and started wondering why she had come up with a question like that.

"I sometimes think about what else I would do but there doesn't seem to be anything that matches this."

Ben couldn't help himself; he had to know.

"You thinking of leaving us?" He was trying to work out what she meant by all this but at the same time trying not to sound too concerned. What would he do without her? And more to the point, it would break his mother's heart if she did leave. *Time to change the subject*, he thought.

They had reached the cattle and Ben had sent a message to his dad.

"Let's get them rounded up before we open the gate and let them go." He had to try and forget about what Emma had said and concentrate on the job at hand. Didn't take them long and soon the cattle were on the way down the road to the next field. It turned out to be a textbook move. On the way back they were talking about how easy it had been and how they had enjoyed it. The look on Emma's face made him smile– he could see how happy she was.

"Nice to see you smile," she suddenly said.

"Hard not to when you are doing what you love to do." He didn't mention that her big smile from ear to ear had something to do with it as well.

It had all gone so smoothly that they had plenty of time

for lunch before the afternoon ride. Once again Ben noticed that his mother wasn't eating a lot. Emma was sat next to him and he gave her a little nudge. She looked at him and then on to Helen and nodded as if she had understood his message.

On the way back up to the yard and far enough away from the house, Emma looked at Ben and said:

"I see what you mean about your mother, Ben. Sorry I didn't get a chance to speak to her after lunch. Maybe you should try and speak to her after dinner tonight."

"Thank you. I was beginning to think it was me and yes, I'll try to but doubt she will tell me anything."

The afternoon rides had quite a few booked in including children that had no experience of riding. What could have turned into a nightmare of a ride was in fact a very nice group of riders. They asked questions but not too many and more to the point, the questions were relevant for once. Afterwards they were all so grateful for the ride and thanked Ben and Emma for the experience. This was something rare these days. Normally when they got back people would get off and leave quickly, leaving him and Emma to do all the work.

"Well, that was fun this afternoon," Emma broke the silence again after the last customer finally had left.

"Yeah, I wish more of the rides could be like this," he replied. She smiled and went to put the last saddle away. As Ben was locking up, Emma hit his arm.

"Hey, what's that for?" He turned his head and saw his father running and waving his arms.

"Go," said Emma. "I'll lock up and meet you at the house."

Ben started walking but before he knew it his legs were running as fast as they could. A million things went through his head.

"What's up, dad?" he shouted.

All he could hear was 'mom something'. As he got closer, he could hear what he said.

"Your mother is on the kitchen floor!"

Ben's legs went up a gear as he sprinted past his father and back to the house. He flew in through the door and found his mother on the kitchen floor looking lifeless.

"Mom!" He shouted and fell to his knees next to her. Emma came in and immediately dialed 911. She grabbed Helen's hand to check if there was a pulse.

"She's alive," Emma looked at Ben who was white as a sheet. "She's gonna be okay, Ben."

Bill had caught up with them and was standing next to Ben.

"What happened?" Ben almost shouted at his father.

"Easy, Ben." Emma said as she got up and went across to Bill.

"Come, sit down here, Bill," she helped him to a chair.

"What happened, Bill?" Emma was holding his hand while he was trying to get his breath back. Bill was clearly in shock and just kept asking if she was dead. Emma tried to reassure him that she was alive and she would be fine.

Helen started to mumble a bit and tried to move. Ben grabbed her hand and at the same time looked to Emma for help.

"Talk to her, tell her she'll be fine and try to keep her calm."

"Just stay still, mom. The ambulance will be here in a minute." Ben was relieved that his mother had started to come round but he knew she was not out of danger yet.

The paramedics arrived after what felt like hours and took over. Ben had to step back and let them do their work. He felt so helpless since all he could do was watch as they prepared Helen for the journey to the hospital. She had regained consciousness but was very confused and all she kept saying was that she had to make dinner.

"Don't worry about that, Helen. I'll do that for you." Emma had come across so Helen could see her and it seemed to settle her down a bit.

Emma turned to Ben.

"Why don't you go with her and then I bring your father in?"

One of the paramedics turned to Bill and asked him if he knew what had happened.

"She just suddenly collapsed – I was next door and heard her shout and then a big bang as she landed on the floor." Helen got taken out on a stretcher and into the ambulance. Emma gave Ben's hand a squeeze and told him to get in.

"See you at the hospital," she put her thumb up to him as the paramedic closed the doors.

Ben couldn't help thinking if his mother was going to die. She looked so helpless on the stretcher wrapped in a blanket. What would he do without her? How was he going to manage the ranch and his father if she wasn't around? All these questions kept going around and around in his head.

"We're here," it was the paramedic that spoke and brought Ben back to the real world again.

He followed them in; Emma and Bill arrived not long after. They were shown into a small room for relatives and told that once the doctors had stabilized and examined Helen, they would come and talk to them.

Ben kept pacing up and down, looking at the floor as he found it impossible to sit still. Bill was sat bent forward with his head in his hands. It was Emma that broke the silence.

"Shall I go and get us some coffee?"

Neither Bill nor Ben replied but she decided to go anyway and returned with three cups of coffee. She had also managed to find some snack bars. She first went and sat next to Bill.

"Here you are," she handed him a coffee.

"Thank you, Emma." Bill took his cup. Ben was still marching up and down not taking notice of anyone so Emma had to get up and grab his hand.

"Now come and sit down, Ben. This'll do you good."

Ben followed her instructions and sat down. After a little while he looked at her.

"Thank you."

"You're welcome." She gave him a smile, one of those that says I am here for you. Ben turned to look at his father.

"We should let John know what happened."

Bill didn't answer but Emma agreed that it wouldn't hurt to call John and tell him what had happened.

"I'll go and do it now." Ben had already got his phone out. He got up and left the room.

He wasn't entirely sure why he had thought of John but Helen was his mother too and deep down he knew that John had a right to know. Now by informing his brother about this there was a high risk that he would be coming home which meant that Ben would have even more things to think about. *Great, as if things weren't bad enough*, he thought – *all I need is John coming home telling me what to do.*

It wasn't that he hated John or had fallen out with him. They had been very close as children but something had changed in their relationship when John moved to New York. Ben had never worked out what the issue was but he had to put that aside for now. Their mother was in hospital, he had no idea what was wrong with her or if she was going to survive and John had a right to know.

He dialed John's number. It rang a few times.

"Hey, brother. Good to hear from you. What's up?"

How did he know that something was up? Ben could hear people in the background; he assumed his brother was out or still at work. No time for small talk so he cut straight to the chase.

"It's mom. She's in hospital. We don't know yet what's wrong."

As Ben was relaying what had happened, he had great difficulty controlling himself. It was as if it just really hit him what had happened. He quickly went back into the room and said, "Emma can explain it all" and he more or less threw the phone at Emma who looked a bit surprised.

"Hi, John," she walked out of the room.

John was confused. Ben had sounded very upset and not made a lot of sense so Emma explained what had happened.

"Do you know how serious it is?"

"Not yet, we are waiting for the doctors to come and tell us."

"Sounds like I better come home, don't you think?"

Emma reassured him that she didn't think it was bad but agreed that it was probably a good idea if he came home to see his parents.

They agreed that he would sort out travel arrangements and head to Montana the next day.

"Thanks, Emma. Tell Ben I'll keep him updated with my travels."

"Okay, will do and I'll make sure he keeps you posted on any news. See you tomorrow."

John wouldn't be there much before the afternoon the next day – the disadvantage of living that far apart. Emma went back in and informed Bill and Ben about what had been arranged.

"Thank you," Bill muttered quietly.

Ben was sat looking at the floor, he didn't want Emma or his father to see the tears that were building up but Emma had spotted them when he threw the phone at her. She walked across and sat down next to him, gave him his phone and put her arm around his shoulders. She didn't say anything; just sat there for a little while.

Ben managed to whisper a little thank you. He had no

idea what he would have done without her there. She had stayed calm through it all. How did she do that?

"It will all be okay," she gave him a little squeeze.

Finally, after what seemed like hours the doctor came in.

"Take it that you're all family?" He asked and Ben quickly replied, "Yes."

"Okay, I'm Dr Hanson and I have come to let you know what we've found out so far." He looked at Bill. "The good news is that she's stable now and you can see her. It looks like she's had a minor stroke which might explain her black-out. Her blood pressure is very high which might be the reason for the stroke. We'll have to keep her in to run some more tests and also get her blood pressure under control. She's awake but very tired and will need some rest so I suggest you come and have a little chat with her and then go home. Should things change overnight, we will of course contact you straight away. Any questions?"

Emma gave Ben's hand a little squeeze and looked at Dr Hanson and said, "Thank you, that is good news."

"Follow me, I'll take you in to her bed. Just to warn you, she is connected up to a lot of wires with various monitors that beep a lot which is normal but can feel overwhelming."

Ben had only heard the stroke bit and all he could think of was that his mom would be in a wheelchair from now on. How were they going to cope with that at home? His head was spinning again.

As they were walking in, Emma could see Ben was struggling. He had this look on his face when he was overthinking things.

"There, you see, she's gonna be fine." Emma had put her arm around him again. He looked at her and smiled.

"Thank you," he said.

"And thank *you* for that little smile," she gave him an extra squeeze before letting go. They had reached Helen's cubicle.

She was half sat up in bed when they walked in and as the doctor had told them, there were a lot of wires connecting her to various monitors that were beeping away. Ben wasn't prepared for the sight; he hadn't really grasped what the doctor had said.

Dr Hanson had noticed Ben's reaction.

"It's okay, these monitors are normal for all new arrivals." He continued, "Mrs. Jackson, I believe these people are your family." He smiled at her, then turned to Bill, Ben and Emma.

"As I said, she's tired and will need to rest so don't make it too long. Any question, please just ask one of the nurses to come and find me."

"Thank you, Dr Hanson," Helen waved to the doctor.

She was so pleased to see them. Bill was on one side of the bed and Ben on the other with Emma behind him. Helen was looking from one to the other.

"They say they want to keep me in for a few days but who's going to help you at home?" She was looking at Ben.

"Don't worry about us, we can manage," said Ben, "the important thing is that you're okay."

"But what about cooking? Neither of you two can cook, I know that for a fact."

"That's not true – I can make sandwiches," Ben smiled at

her and at the same time tried hard not to worry too much about it. At the end of the day, they would work something out.

"Don't worry, Helen, I will make sure they get something to eat." Emma had put her head around Ben so Helen could see her and gave her a reassuring look. She hadn't done a lot of cooking but was pretty sure that between the three of them they would work it out.

"Thank you, Emma. You're such a lovely girl," said Helen as she looked at Ben.

"Now you do as she tells you and don't be rude to her," she gave him a smile then turned to Bill. "The same counts for you, too."

Helen was very tired so they didn't stay for too long but before leaving Emma checked with the nurse what the plan was for the next day in regards to what time would be best to visit. It turned out that they were welcome any time after breakfast so Bill told Helen that he would be back in the morning.

Ben thought for a second whether to tell her about John's plans but decided that it would be better to wait. It would only make his mother feel even more guilty about the whole thing which wasn't what she needed right now.

As they walked to the car Emma reminded Ben that he better send John an update. Apart from Ben relaying his updates and the instant reply from John saying 'thank you' plus his travel plans, not a lot was said as Emma drove them back to the ranch.

In the end, Emma broke the silence.

"I think it'll be good to have John back here for a bit."

Bill didn't say anything and Ben reluctantly said, "Maybe."

Suddenly Ben had realized that his troubles weren't over. Not only was his mother in hospital and the ranch was in some sort of financial trouble – that could be the only reason for the letter - now his brother was coming home as well.

Deep down he was probably a bit jealous or annoyed with how successful John was in whatever he did. He always had great ideas and plans and most of them turned out in his favor as far as Ben knew. On top of that he always seems so happy. *Why couldn't some of my brother's luck come my way?* Ben thought. He could definitely do with some of it now as he felt that life was handing him one problem after another without him being able to sort them out.

{ 3 }

Meanwhile in New York and despite it being Monday, John was out at a reception after work together with his current girlfriend, Melissa. It was going to be one of those weeks where he had something on every evening; in fact, staying in wasn't something he did a lot; always something going on in this wonderful city – the city that never sleeps. If it wasn't work or some sort of reception, he would be dining out with Melissa. Cooking wasn't something he had ever really done and Melissa had zero interest for cooking or staying in either. Having done a bit of modelling she liked to go out so people could notice her.

They had met at the fitness center and it had all started with him suggesting that they should grab a bite after a workout session. He didn't really know a lot about her apart from she was a former model, didn't know what family she had and she had never asked about his.

Ben's call had shocked him a bit and he suddenly remembered he had had a few missed calls from his parents over the last week or so. He hadn't got around to call them back, had been meaning to but work had got in the way.

Ben had sounded pretty upset and John had found it difficult to understand what exactly had happened. He had tried to ask Ben questions but instead of answering Ben had handed the phone to Emma who had explained the reason for the call. Emma had also said that she was pretty sure that his mother was going to be fine. John felt a bit better now he understood what had happened.

Instead, he was more worried about Ben, really. When it came to bad news and crises, his brother wasn't known for being good at handling them. John remembered it clearly how bad Ben had been and how worried about him they all had been. He was relieved that Emma had been there and now was at the hospital with them. He knew that she was a big help but she couldn't do it all. There was only one thing he could and should do - head home to Montana for a visit.

John was trying to remember when he last visited his parents and came to the conclusion that it must have been more than a year ago. He began to feel ashamed that he hadn't been more aware of the time passing but on the other hand, he had been very busy with work, not that it was a good excuse not to visit his parents. Well, he hadn't had a break for a long time and although work was busy at the moment, he could definitely justify a visit to Montana now. His mother might be okay but his gut feeling was that Ben could do with some support.

John went looking for Melissa and found her chatting to a couple of good-looking guys in the bar.

"Hi there, I'm John Jackson," he put his hand out to greet them. They didn't look familiar to him.

"Will you excuse us for a moment?" He turned to Melissa, "I need to speak to you." They left the reception room and stood in the hall where there was less noise. "My brother just called to say that our mother is in hospital after she collapsed at home. They don't know what's wrong with her but I have to go and see her."

He was walking toward the cloakroom to get his coat.

"So, you're leaving now?" Melissa didn't look impressed.

"Yes, I have to sort out a few things and speak to my boss before flying out to Montana tomorrow morning." He suddenly realized he had rather a lot to do before he could go.

"But what about me?" She looked at him like she was the victim in all this. "What am I going to do?"

"I'll get you a taxi and pay for it to take you home." He was a bit taken aback that she didn't seem to care about his mother or his family for that matter.

"So, what about the dinner Wednesday night and the party on the weekend? Will you be back for that?"

Did she not realize where Montana was?

"Highly unlikely as I'm heading more than halfway across the country," he realized that she probably didn't know where Montana was or hadn't listened to what he had said.

"But I can't go on my own. You'll have to be there!" She persisted.

Lost for words, he managed to get her a taxi fairly quickly.

"I will call you when I know more," he said as he opened the door for her. As it drove away, he realized that his relationship with Melissa had to end.

Another taxi pulled up, he jumped in and headed home. On the way he called Tracey, his PA and told her what had happened. She fully agreed with him that he should go; she could keep him up to date with things in the office via email and should he be needed, they could do a video call. She said there was a couple of meetings coming up but they could either be done over the phone or wait until he got back.

"I will book you a flight straight away and email you the details."

"Thank you, Tracey, you're a star. I will call Mr. Patterson now and fill him in."

Boy, was he glad he had her; if there was anyone that could sort out problems, it was Tracey.

Back home he went to the fridge, grabbed a beer and sat down. Well, that wasn't how he had planned the day to end or the week to start for that matter.

One of the big disadvantages with living that far away was the time it took to travel which was not helped by no direct flights to western Montana from New York. Tracey had sent him a message with his flight details. She had managed to book a ticket where the waiting time for the connecting flight wasn't too long. It meant that he could be at the ranch in the afternoon. Now that was sorted, he dialed Mr. Patterson's number and to John's relief, he answered.

"Good evening, John. What can I do for you?"

John felt really bad about ringing him so late even though they were very good friends but this was kind of an emergency so he had no other choice as he was leaving first thing in the morning.

"Good evening, Mr. Patterson, and sorry for disturbing you so late in the day."

"Not a problem. What can I do for you?"

John went on to explain about the family situation and his need to take some leave.

"John, if I know you right, you haven't had any time off for a long time so take the time you need. This is your family and they're important to you."

"Thank you so much for your understanding."

"I trust you'll organize things with Tracey so your appointment can be rescheduled."

John confirmed that that had already happened and he would keep both Tracey and Mr. Patterson informed regarding to what was happening.

"Now don't rush to get back here. Your family is important to you. I know this from personal experience and they need you now."

"I'll try not to."

Mr. Patterson wished him good luck. John sat for a while thinking of what he had said and was thankful that he had a boss that understood his needs. Not all bosses would do the same thing. In his line of work a lot of them would or did put work before family. And in some ways John had fallen into that trap too. Maybe this was a bit of a wake-up call for him. Maybe the time had come for him to take a good look at his life and his priorities.

He got up and went looking for his travel bag. Time to get packing. John wasn't sure what to bring or for how long. He decided that enough for a week or so and should he need more, there were shops there. He then made sure that he had packed all the relevant work documents that he would need in order to be able to work from Montana.

Once done, he checked his phone for messages – one from Ben: "Mum fine, minor stroke, needs to stay in for some more tests". John replied with a "thank you" and thought that it was so typical of Ben, he was never one for using many words – a man of few words like their father, that was his brother.

He sent Ben his travel details including that he would hire a car at the airport so that Ben didn't have to think of collecting him. It would also mean that he was freer; he could come and go without having to rely on someone taking him.

That's it, all done and as it was going to be an early start in the morning it was time for him to hit the pillows. John had one last glance around his apartment. No, there wasn't anything else he needed to take care of.

Back at the ranch, it was clear to see that they had left it in a bit of a hurry. Bill went and sat down at the kitchen table. *He looks so lost*, Ben thought as he and Emma were trying to sort out the mess.

"Do you two want something to eat?"

It was past normal dinner time but Emma thought they ought to have something to eat and it would maybe break the silence.

"I'm not really hungry. What about you, dad?" Ben looked at his father.

Bill looked up and hadn't heard the question.

"What? Sorry, didn't hear what you said, son." He looked really sad so Emma went to sit down next to him and took his hand.

"You okay, Bill?" She was a bit concerned for him; he was obviously in shock. He looked at her.

"What am I going to do?" There were tears in his eyes and Emma gave him a big hug.

"It's all gonna be okay, Bill. Helen is in a good place; the doctors will sort her out and she'll be home in no time. I'm pretty sure of that. Now, how about something to drink and a little sandwich?" Emma got up and decided that rather waiting for them to say yes she would make them both and herself a sandwich.

"Bill, do you want cheese in yours?" Emma looked at him.

He nodded. She then turned her attention to Ben.

"And what about you? Same for you?"

Ben wasn't really hungry but decided that it was probably a good idea to have a bit to eat.

"Yes, please," he went and sat down next to his father.

Now Ben wasn't normally one for showing his feelings but he couldn't resist putting his arms around his father and giving him a little hug. He didn't really know what to say. Yeah, what do you say to a man whose wife of over thirty years had just been rushed off to hospital? He had never been in that situation before.

He was saved by Emma who had done the sandwiches and drinks. Not a word was said as they tucked in to each of their sandwich.

"Anyone want more?" Emma broke the silence. As she got no reply, she got up and started to clear up. "So, do we know what's happening tomorrow? I mean, are there any rides booked?"

"Don't know. You better go and check the diary and I'll

check the phone." Ben had got up and was helping with the cleaning up. Bill was still sat at the table.

"I don't think there is but I can't remember."

"That's okay. I'll go and have a look." Emma put her hand on Bill's shoulder as she passed him.

"Be right back." She soon returned and sat down next to him. "Nope, nothing booked in for tomorrow but there is one for the next day. Any messages on the phone, Ben?"

Ben had been to check, there wasn't any. In some ways, he was relieved that they didn't have any booking for the next day. With all the things that had happened, he couldn't face dealing with people. And no one knew how Helen was going to be. What if she had another episode overnight? Also, John was arriving; no doubt he would have all sorts of questions for him. Then there was the matter of where John was going to sleep. Ben hadn't been upstairs for a while so he didn't know if there was a room free. He would have to check that before his brother arrived.

Bill suddenly started to panic.

"I need to do the chickens." He started to get up but Emma was quicker.

"I'll pop out and put them away."

In all the things that had gone on they had completely forgotten about the chickens. The last thing they needed right now was losing Helen's pride and joy – her chickens. Emma returned with a smile on her face.

"All sorted and safely put away."

"Thank you, Emma. Well, I think I'll go to bed." Bill had

got up from the table now and Ben couldn't help thinking that his father looked old.

"I'll be going to the hospital first thing in the morning so I won't be here to help." Bill was heading in next door.

"That's okay, dad. We'll manage without you." Ben looked at Emma as if to say 'what do I do now'.

"Don't you think it'd be best you stay here tonight or would you rather I stayed with him? I don't really think he should be here on his own."

Ben hadn't thought of that but she was right; he couldn't leave his father on his own. He was still in shock.

"Dad, I'll sleep here tonight so you're not on your own."

"I'll be fine but if you insist." Bill had sat down and turned on the TV.

Now that it was just the two of them in the kitchen, Emma went across to Ben and gave him a big hug. She knew he didn't like close contact but he really looked like he needed one. At first Ben didn't really know what to do, it had been a long time since he last had a hug like that from anyone else than his mother. All he could manage was:

"Thank you for all your help today, not sure what I'd have done without you."

"Glad I was here. Are you sure you're gonna be okay?" She looked directly at him.

"I'll be fine. Will need to just pop down and get a few things from my place."

"Well, in that case I think I'll head home then." Emma popped her head in to Bill who was still sat watching TV.

"Good night, Bill. Hope you get some sleep. And don't

worry about the chickens – I'll take care of them. If you don't mind, I might take some eggs home to mom, she loves baking."

"Help yourself, and thank you for your help today."

Emma headed for the door.

"Call me if anything happens but I honestly think your mom is going to be fine."

Ben looked at her and then went in to his father.

"Dad, I'm just gonna get a few things from my place. Be right back." He followed Emma out.

"I'll be back tomorrow morning early and then we can plan how to attack the day. Okay?" Emma had opened the car and was getting in it. Ben put his hand on the door.

"Thank you so much for your help today, Emma. It is much appreciated; not sure we would have coped without you."

"Don't worry about it. We got through it. Night, night," she started the car and Ben closed her door.

He waved to her as she drove off down the drive towards the main road, and then headed for his house. Once inside, he sat down. It was as if he had walked straight into a brick wall and he couldn't hold back the tears any longer. His head was hurting, it felt like it was spinning out of control – so many things had happened. He had no idea how bad things were going to get and what he was going to do about it. He had a feeling that his mother's illness was just the tip of the iceberg. Something told him that there was something a lot worse about to happen.

And then there was Emma who was the solid rock, the

one that had stayed calm, the one who kept saying that it would all be okay. How could she know that? He was full of frustration, almost angry with her for being so positive but at the same time he felt like she was the only one that could help him right now, but how?

All these feelings... He had no idea how to handle them or what to do about them. One thing was sure, he had to get back up to the house. Emma was right; there was no way he could leave his father alone in the house overnight. *Come on, you are a grown man, pull yourself together*. He got up and went into the bedroom and grabbed a few things. *Well, tomorrow can only be better,* he thought as he headed up the drive to the house.

By the time he got back to the house Bill had gone to bed. Ben took his stuff up to what used to be his bedroom. It had turned into a spare room where things got put in out of the way but the bed was still there and made. He went along and opened the door to what used to be his brother's room. His mother had kept it just the way it was when John left all those years ago. And yes, the bed was made too like it was waiting for him to come home. *Mom must miss him a lot,* Ben thought and wondered if John realized that.

Back downstairs again he went to the fridge, grabbed a beer and then headed to the office. He wanted to have a look at the diary and see what was booked in for the coming week. As he picked it up from the desk, the letter from the Bank fell out and landed on the floor. In all the madness of the day he had completely forgotten about the letter. He froze for a second, looked at it and then reached down to pick it up. Now holding it in his hands he wasn't sure what to do about it. Should he read it or not? Would he be able to handle what it said? On the other hand, would he be able to sleep knowing he had found it but not read it? No, he decided that it would be best if he knew what it said. He was still pretty convinced that it was bad news.

As he sat down in the chair, he noticed that it hadn't even been opened. Ben had turned the envelope around and the return address told him that he was right; it was from the Bank. How could they had ignored a letter from the Bank? He opened the envelope carefully, took the letter out and unfolded it.

This *was* bad news. He read it through twice to be sure he had read it correctly. It was to do with the mortgage his parents had taken out a few years ago when a storm had damaged the roof on the main house badly and some of the other buildings. The repair was costly which had forced them reluctantly to take out the mortgage with the Bank. The letter that Ben was holding, was a reminder – actually a second reminder the Bank had sent - of the agreement they had signed. It appeared that they had fallen behind with the payments by a few months and now the Bank was asking for a meeting to discuss how they planned to make the missed payments. If that wasn't enough, it went on to say that if they weren't able to make the payment by the end of the month, the Bank would shut them down and sell the ranch. Ben glanced at the diary; today's date was June 12. They had about three weeks to try and find a solution.

This was bad, very bad indeed. Ben kept staring at the letter, reading it over and over. Why had they not told him anything about the struggle to make the payments? And why had they not replied to the first letter the bank had sent them? If he had known earlier, he might have been able to find a solution, not that he had any ideas of how. Deep down he knew his parents were too proud to admit that they had financial problems and needed help but still. They could lose everything now.

So many things went through his head and in the end, he got his phone out and looked for his brother's number. He looked at his watch. No, it would be far too late to call John. He went back to look for Emma's number. Should he call her? He decided not to as it would mean he would have to tell her everything and he wasn't ready for that.

As he sat there reflecting on the day's events and the fact that he was right about things getting worse, he wondered if John knew about the mortgage and the payment issues – probably not. Maybe John would be able to help them out with the payment. No, he didn't want to go there; being rescued by his brother was like a complete failure on his part. It would only lead to John starting to get involved in running the ranch and telling him what to do. What would he know about running a ranch? No, this was his ranch or at least that was the plan and therefore his problem. At the end of the day John was the one who chose to move away and left them to run it.

It was safe to say that it had not been one of Ben's better days – it had started well but the last few hours were like a nightmare where the problems kept coming without him being able to sort them out, and from which there was no escape.

He started to have a look around to try and work out what they had in terms of income but he didn't really have a clue where to look. His mother was the one that was in charge of the office work but she would be out of action for a little while. Somehow, he would have to try and work it out. He decided that he would contact the Bank in the morning once his father had left for the hospital and try to arrange a meeting. Maybe, just maybe they would be able to see things from his side, the circumstance he was in and then give him some more time. He wasn't hopeful but at least he could try. The next issue was how he was going to hide it all from his brother. He had to try and put on a brave face and act like all was okay.

It was rather late now, nearly midnight so he decided to go to bed and try and get some sleep. Maybe he would wake up in the morning and it would all have been a very bad dream.

{ 4 }

As Ben woke up it took him a little while to work out where he was and suddenly it all came back to him. He quickly got up, dressed and headed down to the kitchen. No sign of his dad and his car was still parked out in front of the house next to his truck. Ben wondered if he ought to go and check on him. He couldn't remember the last time he had got up before his parents so he headed back upstairs, gave a gentle knock on the door followed by opening it a small gap. Bill turned his head and mumbled,

"Hello."

"Just checking you're okay, dad. I'll get breakfast ready."

"Alright, I'll be there in a minute."

"No rush, take your time." Ben felt a bit of relief. Now he had to try and sort out breakfast which he knew he was quite capable of doing. As he was making coffee, he saw Emma's car come up the drive and it brought a smile to his face. *Seriously what is with that girl*, he thought. Suddenly he remembered he had to unlock the back door so she could get in.

"Morning! How's everybody?" Emma walked into the kitchen looking happy with fresh eggs she had collected on the way in when letting the hens out.

"We're okay. No calls from the hospital so I take it mom is okay."

"That's good news, Ben. I told you she'll be fine. Have you heard from your brother?"

"Not this morning but he should be here after lunch."

"Bill still asleep? Is he okay?"

"Yeah, I just checked, he'll be here in a minute."

"Well, looks like you got it all under control then," she smiled at him and went to get some plates for the toast.

"I bought some fresh bread for your breakfast."

"Thank you, that was very kind of you. Hope these scrambled eggs are okay. What do you think?" he showed her the pan and smiled.

"Looks pretty good to me. Sure, it'll be fine," Emma said as she was getting the table ready.

Ben's phone made a noise, it was a message from his brother.

"John says he has landed in Minneapolis."

"That's good to know. Can't wait to see what he thinks of outdoor work. Maybe we should try and get him back riding again, what do you think he would say to that?"

Ben didn't answer straight away as he was trying to work out what she meant by that. He checked to see if his father was on his way down yet before he answered.

"Not sure if I am really looking forward to him coming home."

"What happened between you two?"

Before Ben could answer the question, Bill walked into the kitchen.

"Morning, Emma, you're here early."

"Morning, Bill. Yeah, wanted to make sure that you got

out of bed and had some breakfast before you head to the hospital." She gave him a big smile.

Ben was pleased to see his father. It meant that he couldn't really answer Emma's question. The fact was that he didn't have an answer, he couldn't explain what had happened between him and John.

"No calls from the hospital, dad, so mom must be fine."

Ben hoped that by changing the subject the whole John issue would go away for now. There was plenty of other things that needed his attention right now.

"Good," Bill replied. "I'll head there once I've had my breakfast."

"Do you want one of us to take you in?" Ben suddenly thought that maybe it would be better if either him or Emma drove him in.

"No, I'll be fine, son. Besides, you have plenty to do here."

That was a bit of a relief for Ben as it meant he could get on with a few things before John would turn up.

"Okay. I'll come in later together with John once he's here."

"I'd suggest you call and ask them how she is and what their plans are regarding seeing doctors," Emma looked at them both. "That way you know what's happening and when would be a good time to visit."

"Good idea." Ben got the phone and dialed the number. It rang a couple of times before a lady answered it. Ben explained who he was and asked how his mother was and if there was a plan for the day.

"Thanks a lot. My father will be in soon if you could be

kind to let her know." He hung up and relayed what he had been told. She had a very good night's sleep, there was a couple of scans booked for the morning and Bill was welcome to come along. He looked relieved to hear that. Him and Helen hadn't been apart for this long since they got married 35 years ago.

"Well, I better be on my way then," Bill got up but before he left, they all agreed that Ben would bring John in once he had arrived and that would be when Helen would find out.

Now with his father going to the hospital it gave Ben an opportunity to spend some time in the office. He needed to try and work out how to approach the bank issue and preferably before anyone else found out. If only he had someone he could talk to – most of the time he was happy to sort things out on his own but this was like climbing Mount Everest as he had absolutely no idea of where to start.

He looked at Emma; maybe he should talk to her. But what could she do – she was younger than him and what did she know about finances and running a business?

"Well," Emma broke the silence. "What do you want me to do today?" She looked at Ben.

"Well, we better get out and do things." Ben got up from his chair. He had decided that a ride out to check the cattle could maybe help him clear his brain. Parts of him wanted to talk to Emma about his discovery but the other part didn't want to involve her in his problems. He had never found it easy to open up and ask for help. "Let's saddle up a couple of horses and go for a ride." He went to find his father to ask him to lock the house when he left for the hospital as they were heading out now.

It was another beautiful morning. Ben loved the refreshing feeling of the air in the morning.

"Boy, am I glad we don't have any rides today. Don't think I could cope with all the questions," he heard himself saying as they walked. Emma looked at him and smiled.

"Yeah, been a crazy twenty-four hours really but this will help you, I'm pretty sure of that. It'll be a good way to clear the mind and reflect on it all."

She sounded so cheerful that it was difficult for Ben not to smile a little. They had reached the yard and got a couple of horses in for the ride.

"We better try and work out a plan for the next couple of weeks. I don't think your mom will be allowed to do any work. She'll need to rest and take it easy when she gets home." Emma was already getting on her horse. Ben looked at her and thought to himself that she had no idea about how big the issue was.

"Yeah, definitely need a plan," he said and got on his horse.

Soon they were on their way– heading up the road with the mountains ahead of them. This was exactly what Ben needed. Deep down he knew it would only be a temporary break – he would have to get back and face the issue but right now he was going to fill his lungs with fresh air like a battery getting charged.

Emma broke the silence. She had spotted a couple of deer just in the field on her side.

"So, Ben... How bad are things?"

Ben ought to have known that Emma wouldn't be able to stay quiet for long but it still caught him off guard.

"What do you mean?" He was trying to sound surprised.

"Well, I might be young but I know that we haven't been that busy this year. The other day I walked into the kitchen and your parents – they hadn't heard me coming- were arguing over whether to tell you or not, something about a letter from the Bank. I didn't get all of it and felt a bit ashamed that I'd listened in so I made the door close harder and said hello. They thought I'd just walked in. They have no idea that I heard what they were talking about. And please don't tell them."

So, she actually knew that there was something wrong. Why hadn't she said anything to him? How much did she know? And why had his parents not done anything about it when they had the first letter? Ben could feel the anger building inside him.

"Why didn't you tell me?" He said it in a way that made him sound quite angry and regretted straight away the tone of his voice. "Sorry, I didn't mean it like that. And no, I won't tell them. In fact, I was going to speak to you about it hence the reason for the ride. So, when did you hear this?"

"It was the day before yesterday and honestly I wanted to but just couldn't find the right time and place. Sorry."

In some way this was a big relief for Ben. The fact that she knew would make it easier for him to talk to her about it.

"Well, I am glad you have told me and to answer your

question I had no idea about it until last night." He told her what he had read in the letter last night.

"I am so sorry to hear this, Ben. But if anyone can work it out, it'll be you. Just remember that I'm here and happy to help and you have John coming too."

Yeah, he did have John coming but he would rather try and sort it out himself if he could.

They had reached the field and spent some time looking over the cattle. Ben then suggested they rode down to his spot along the river. As they reached it, they got off the horses and went and sat down. It was definitely warming up now, no cloud in the sky. The river was fairly quiet but then again there hadn't been any significant rain for a while.

"So, what are you going to do?" Emma looked at Ben who was staring at the river. He turned his head to look at her. *Beautiful eyes*, he thought. *Why have I not noticed them before?*

"Well, I don't really know. First, I have to take a look at the books and try and work out what the situation is. Will do that when we get back, since dad's out of the house."

"What about John? He'd be able to help you."

"It has crossed my mind but I'd rather do this on my own," he had turned his head back to the river.

"But you are going to tell him about it?"

"Yeah, I will but I don't need to be rescued by him." Ben got up. Emma sensed that he was very uncomfortable talking about John.

"Look, I know you want to do it on your own but it wouldn't hurt to see if he maybe has some ideas." She got on her horse and rode up next to him. Knowing Ben's history,

Emma decided that she had to be on extra alert, she didn't want to risk Ben starting to 'shut down' and not talking to anyone like last time. "Ben, you are an amazing guy and I'm pretty sure that you'll get this sorted but it will be easier if you would let us help you."

Ben didn't say anything but deep down he knew she was right. But somehow, he found it very hard to ask for help – to him it felt like he had failed. They rode home in silence.

Ben was cross with himself. He had no reason to be angry with Emma – she hadn't done anything wrong. Perhaps she was right about John but he just couldn't bring himself to do it. It would be like a massive failure on his part. What had really happened between him and John? They had been so close when growing up. John had a successful career in New York now and here he was, at home busy running the ranch into the hands of the Bank without knowing it.

They had reached the yard and Emma grabbed the reins from him.

"Here, let me take care of the horses then you can go and start your search." He had no options but to agree.

"Are you sure?" He wasn't looking forward to do it but knew he had to.

"Yes, go. I'll pop in before I head home," she smiled.

Emma knew Ben enough to know that he would be trying to avoid it if he could.

"Okay," he said and started slowly walking towards the house.

Now, where to start? He had reached the office and sat down. It took him a little while before he had found everything. From what he could see they had only fallen behind with a couple of months back in the early spring. There was a couple of letters from the Bank and it was clear that his parents hadn't reacted to any of them. Maybe that was why the Bank's last letter was so sharp. But this was their business and they hadn't done anything wrong apart from not reaching out to the Bank after the first letter.

Well, he had to find a way out of it. At least he would have some cattle to sell a bit later in the summer which would bring in some cash. There was no way around it; he had to try and make an appointment with the Bank. And maybe if he explained the situation, they would be willing to give him some time to try and work out how to boost the income. Perhaps if he took a part time job somewhere, he could do deliveries for the feed store– that could help.

Emma had finished everything and popped her head in to the office.

"How're you doing?"

"Well, it's not looking good. Looks like my parents tried to ignore the Bank unfortunately. But now that I know what happened, I'll try and get an appointment with them later this week and take it from there."

"Good plan," she said. "Look, do you need me more today?"

"Don't think so," Ben looked at her. "Do you have something in mind?"

"Nah, I'll head home. Need to do some shopping and I thought I'd swing by and see your mom as well."

"Can't argue with that. See you tomorrow?"

"Yeah... now will you be able to do the chickens tonight?" She had put her hands on his shoulders.

"Yeah, I'll try and remember," he had turned the chair around a bit. "Thanks for listening and sorry if I sounded a bit angry earlier."

"No problem. I fully understand, I just don't want you to head down that slippery slope where you keep everything to yourself. You know that's not good." She bent down to give him a little hug as he sat there in the chair.

He watched her as she walked through the house. She was right again. What would he do without her? He looked at the time. Bill could be home any time soon so he had better get on and contact the Bank. Before he had a chance to change his mind, he had dialed the number. It rang a few times before a nice lady answered.

"Ben Jackson here from Jackson Ranch. I was wondering if it was possible to get a meeting with Mr. Miles, the bank manager?"

The nice lady put him through to the manager's PA who asked for the reason for a meeting. He explained that it was regarding a letter they had received. *Surely, she should know,* he thought. She probably typed the letter in the first place.

"How about tomorrow morning at 11 o'clock?"

"Yeah, that'll be okay," he replied, thanked her and hung up.

What have I just done? He sat back in the chair; his legs felt like jelly. Well, less than twenty-four hours away which meant that he would soon know if he had a chance.

Next thing was whether to tell his parents about it but

now didn't seem like the right time to do so. Adding stress to his mother was not what the doctor had ordered. And his father would be too occupied with her in hospital that he wouldn't think about contacting the Bank. So, it was best that Ben would have the meeting with the bank, explain the situation and hopefully buy some time. Then he could let them know. In the meantime, he had to try and stay calm.

His phone went ping; another message from John telling him that he had landed, got the car and was heading to the ranch. Ben replied with an "okay". *Oh, joy.* That would mean he could be here within the next hour or so. Well, time to grab a bite and get his feelings under control. He had just sat down when Bill returned home.

"How is she?" Ben asked as soon as his father walked into the kitchen. He realized that he hadn't really had time to think about his mother and whether she was okay or not.

"Fine." Bill looked tired. "Still got a few tests to run. Emma dropped by so I thought I'd go home for a spell. I could use a nap since I didn't sleep that well last night. Haven't heard anything about John. Do we know when he's coming?"

"Within the next hour or so." Ben got up. "Can I make you a sandwich, dad?"

"Yes, please."

"I'll take John to see mom once he's unpacked and ready. Is she up for it?"

"Yeah. She's still a bit tired, didn't get that much sleep last night. She complained that there was so much noise and the nurses kept coming in to check her blood pressure. I wonder how long he plans to stay for?"

Ben had to think for a second what his father was on about.

"Oh, you mean John. He didn't say. Why?"

"Just thought it'd be nice to have him around for a while. We haven't seen him for such a long time. Do you think he'd ever consider moving back here?"

"I have no idea but doubt it. If I understand it right his world is in business, shares and banking – pretty sure that there's more of that in New York than around here. Don't you think?"

"Yeah, probably but would just be nice if we could see more of him; your mom would like that."

This was the most Ben had heard his father talk about John in a very long time and he was beginning to feel slightly uncomfortable about the direction the conversation was heading so he decided to change the subject quickly.

"Have the doctors said anything about what's wrong with mom?"

"No, the scan this morning was fine but they still have a few other things they wanna do. They said they hope to give us the results tomorrow."

"Well, whatever it is she's gonna have to take it easy for a while, I think."

"Yeah, you're right, son and that's not going to be easy. You know what she's like."

"Yes, I do."

Ben knew his mother well enough to know that it was going to be a challenge but he had a plan that involved Emma.

He hadn't actually spoken to her about it yet but was pretty sure she would be up for it.

"Well, what if I ask Emma if she could help her, do you think mom would mind? We're not that busy with the rides at the moment anyway and if I need an extra set of hands, John can ride." As he said the last bit, he looked at his father to see what reaction he got, if any.

"Sounds like a plan. You know how she loves having Emma around."

Well, he didn't seem to react to the 'not very busy' part. How could he not? Ben could feel the anger growing inside him so he decided that he had better get outside and try to gain some control over his feelings.

"Just gonna go down to my place for a while. Be back soon. Okay?"

"Yeah, fine by me." Bill had finished his lunch and was heading next door.

Once outside Ben took a couple of deep breaths and then headed down to his place. Once inside he thought for a second and then dialed Emma's number.

"How's it going?" The sound of the happy voice at the other end immediately had a positive effect on him.

"Okay," he went on to tell her about the meeting and his thoughts about her helping his mom out and his father's questions about John. He stopped short of telling her why he had walked out of the house just now.

"Not a problem, Ben, you know I got your back. But is that the reason why you called?"

He had to tell her about his reaction to the fact that his father hadn't said anything.

"Ben, remember that he's had a lot of things happening and I don't think it has crossed his mind. Now why don't we keep this between us until you've seen the bank tomorrow and then we can plan the next step."

"Sounds like a plan and sorry, I just had to speak to someone."

"You did the right thing by calling me and you know you can always talk to me. By the way your mother looks a lot better today. She's looking forward to see you later."

Ben thanked her and said he would keep her updated on the afternoon's event. He got changed so he would be ready to head into town once his brother had arrived.

{ 5 }

"John's here!" Bill called out.

Ben was sat in the office, having just taken another booking and hadn't noticed the car pulling up outside the house. He got up and headed out together with his father to greet his brother and help him carry his bags in.

"Good to see you, son." Bill's eyes glistened tears as he gave his oldest son a big hug.

"Nice to see you too, dad." John was slightly taken aback by his father's action. The brothers weren't used to seeing their father showing his feelings like that.

"Good to see you, big brother." Ben gave John a squeeze.

"And hello little brother even though you are bigger and look stronger than me," John laughed.

"We already had lunch. Are you hungry? You look like you could do with some food." Bill looked at his oldest son like he was looking at the cattle. He then went on. "Don't they have food in New York?"

"I'm alright. I grabbed a sandwich before getting in the car but I could do with a cup of coffee."

"You look like you could do with a bit of sleep if you don't mind me saying so."

Ben thought his brother looked rather tired which was kind of understandable as John had been travelling since before sunrise and through time zones. But apart from that, he looked to be in pretty good shape for someone sat in an office all day long.

"Yeah, somewhat an early start for me but some coffee will keep me going for a bit. Maybe we could grab one at the hospital. How's mom holding up? Is she okay?"

"Yeah, dad's been with her all morning. He came back about an hour ago." Ben filled John in on what Bill had told him.

"My plan is to take you there this afternoon. By the way, we haven't told her that you were coming home; you know what she's like."

"I know. Sounds like a good plan. Is dad coming too?"

"He'll be there later after his nap."

"Okay," John turned his head and looked around the place. "Looks like nothing has changed here."

"Yeah, no need to change when it's working." Ben bent down to pick up his brother's bags. "Come on, let's get your bags upstairs." He was trying to ignore John's comment about the place and hoped that by changing the subject there wouldn't be any more comments or worse – questions. Bill had already gone in and was heading for his nap. Once Ben had got the bags inside the door of John's old bedroom, he put them down on the floor. "Don't think this has changed since you left."

"I know. I do feel bad that I haven't been home more often but you know what it's like when you get caught up in things and time just flies."

"I know... Well, I'll leave you to get ready."

Ben left his brother to unpack and headed downstairs

again. John seemed so relaxed and pleased to see them which had surprised Ben a little. Maybe it was just him that had an issue or maybe there wasn't one but just something that Ben somehow had got into his head. In fact, part of him felt somewhat relieved now that John was here, not sure why but it felt good.

John came back down fairly quickly having changed to some more relaxed clothes. Ben couldn't help thinking how smart his brother looked and couldn't help wondering if John had brought any clothes suitable for riding. The thought made him smile.

"What are you so happy about?" John had noticed the smile.

"Oh nothing, just wondered if you had brought any work clothes with you, that's all. And just to warn you, dad is likely to ask how long you're staying for."

"No, haven't really brought any work clothes – kind of hoping I can fit into something here if need to. And thanks for the warning. I haven't really set a time frame. Got plenty of holiday to take; apparently I'm not good at taking time off." John smiled.

Well, you are right there, Ben thought to himself and replied.

"Yeah, I think it's safe to say that it's been noted here." Ben carried on telling John some of the questions he had had from their father earlier.

"Well, I'm thinking of some changes but can't say anything yet. Please don't tell mom and dad."

"I won't. Coffee?" The last thing he needed now was their

parents getting some kind of false hope that his brother would be coming back.

"Nah, I'd prefer to get one at the hospital if you don't mind. I'm ready; shall we go?"

"No problem," Ben was a little surprised by John's hurry to get to the hospital. Why the rush? He was the one that hadn't been home for over a year, he was the one that rarely spoke to their parents on the phone. And now he couldn't get to the hospital quick enough. Maybe, just maybe his brother was feeling guilty or maybe the possibility of losing his mother had made him realize that his family wasn't immortal.

Ben hadn't really thought about it in that way himself until now but what would have happened if his father hadn't been in when his mother had her fall? What would have happened then? Ben could feel his stomach turning and he tried very hard to push those thoughts out of his head. He couldn't be thinking of that now.

Pull yourself together, man. Now is not the time to show weakness, he kept telling himself.

"Yeah, I'm ready, let's go." They headed out to Ben's truck. Bill would be in later so John would have the option to either come back with Ben or John could stay and then come home with their father. Ben had to come back and sort things out especially as he had given Emma the afternoon off.

Before John jumped in Ben had a quick look to see if the seat was clean, this was after all a working truck and he wouldn't want John's nice clothes to get dirty.

"Looks okay. We better be on the way then." He went around to the driver's side. As he started the truck, he was trying to work out how he could avoid John asking him too many questions about the ranch and the business. The only thing he could think of to avoid it would be to ask John lots of questions about his life in New York. He had to have something to tell being as he was too busy to come home and visit them.

"So do you have any serious girlfriend in New York?" Not that Ben really cared about that but he had to start somewhere.

"Not really. I'm quite busy with work which doesn't leave me with much time for that kind of socializing." John went on to tell Ben all about his work, about Melissa and her reaction to his reason for going to Montana. "I can safely say that I won't be seeing her again," John looked out of the window and continued. "On the way across the country I realized that I've been so caught up in work that I haven't paid attention to the people around me. I've realized that I don't actually have any, what I would call, serious friends, you know friends you need when there is a crisis. Well, I have my boss and my PA but that isn't really the same because they are work colleagues."

"What do you mean?" Ben wasn't sure what to say but felt like he had to say something.

"You know when something happens like mom being rushed to hospital and you need a good friend to talk to. My PA is pretty good; she's pretty understanding – almost like a mother to me but I don't have any friends outside work."

For a second Ben didn't know what to say. John's comment about his PA being like a mother to him had shocked him. What exactly did he mean by that? What about his real mother? He could feel the resentment towards John building inside him.

"Would you seriously consider moving back to Montana?" It hadn't been Ben's intention to ask such a direct question but he didn't really know what else to say right now. The comment about the PA was still occupying his mind. John had mentioned about a change a couple of times now and it would be good to know if he was serious about it was Ben's thought. Yet again, John surprised him with his answer.

"Yeah, it's crossed my mind alright and I won't rule it out. There comes a point where you get to a crossroad and you have to decide which way to go. I have achieved a lot and reached as far as I can where I am now so maybe it would be time to think about where to go next." He paused for a moment. "And since your call yesterday and the following chat with my boss I've been thinking a lot about what's important in my life. I know I haven't been at home a lot over the last few years and I am truly sorry about that. Last night I realized that mom and dad are not getting any younger and it isn't fair to ask them to move to me or for that matter to leave you to look after them. So, why not?"

"It's a big step to take." Ben looked at him and he couldn't help thinking that his brother looked like he was being very open and honest about it all. "Do you think you could cope with the quiet life here? I mean, it would be totally different to what you're used to and what about work? What would you do here?"

"Well, I don't know. In terms of work, I can in principle

work from anywhere. Who knows? The company might even set up an office here. So far, I plan to stay for a couple of weeks and I might have a look around to see if I could find something that would interest me. Now enough about me, what about you? Any girlfriend I should know about here?" John looked at him with a big smile.

"Nope, haven't really got time for friends at the moment."

"What about Emma?"

"What about her?" The sudden change of subject had caught Ben out. He hadn't had a chance to prepare himself for those kinds of questions. Luckily, they had arrived at the hospital.

"I bet she's still pretty good-looking and I know mom and dad still love her," John looked closely at Ben and was pretty sure Ben was hiding something. He hadn't forgotten about what happened to him some years ago but surely, he would have moved on by now. Well, now wasn't the time to start asking more questions as they were about to enter the hospital. Instead, he wanted to make sure that Ben understood that all the talk about him moving back to Montana had to stay between the two of them for now.

"Ben, I'd really appreciate if we don't say anything about my future plans. I don't want mom and dad to get too excited, especially with mom here."

Ben could only agree with that. "No, you're right. I won't say anything. I'll leave it to you to tell them when you feel the time is right. It is after all your life and not mine."

They entered the building and went straight to the small

café in the lobby to get a coffee. As they were stood there waiting to be served, a woman walked in.

"Hey, isn't that the Jackson boys?"

Both Ben and John turned around to see who it was that had recognized them. It took them both a few seconds to work out who the young, rather good-looking, lady was. John was a second quicker than Ben.

"Hey, Maria! How are you?" John put his hand out to greet her but Maria went further and gave him a big hug. Then she went on to Ben and did the same to him.

"Hi, Maria. Long time no see." Ben wasn't sure what else to say. He and Maria had been very close friends back when they were at school together but somehow, they had lost touch.

"So, what are you two doing here?" She looked at them both.

"We came to see mom, she had a minor fall yesterday."

Ben didn't feel the need to elaborate too much on what had happened.

"Oh no, I hope she's okay." Maria looked a bit shocked to hear that.

"What are you doing here?" It was John's turn to say something.

"Just visiting a friend who's had a baby girl," she waved a pink present and smiled. "How long are you in town for, John? I thought you lived in New York?"

"Yeah, I do but I've come home to see the family. Here for a couple of weeks, I think."

Ben noticed that John was struggling to take his eyes off her.

"We should meet up over a coffee and have a catch-up while you're in town." Maria then turned to Ben and looked at him. "You haven't changed a bit. Still pretty handsome if I may say so. And why have we not stayed in touch?"

Ben could feel his cheeks blushing a bit. He found it very difficult to handle comments like that.

"Tell you what. Is Emma still working for you, Ben? If so, why don't we all meet up and have coffee together one day? It'd be so great to catch up with y'all." Maria looked at her phone. "Gosh, I better go. Here's my card, give me a call when you're free and we can arrange it." She handed her card to John.

"Okay," both replied – lost for words.

"Give my love to your mom, and really good to see you guys." She gave them both a hug and headed towards the maternity ward.

"Well, well, well, she hasn't changed a lot." John was watching her as she went through the door.

"No," Ben was still lost for words, "well, apart from looking even better I'd say."

"I wonder what she does now?" John looked at her card. "Manager, it says. Looks like she works at the tourist shop next to the hotel in the center of town."

They grabbed their coffee and headed up to see their mother.

Helen was half sat up in bed dozing off. It had been a tiring day with all the scans and testing plus the lack of sleep from the night before. She did hear the knock on the door but hadn't quite got herself together before Ben entered.

"Sorry, mom. Did I wake you up?"

"No, it's okay, son. I was just trying to catch up on a bit of sleep from last night."

"I brought someone with me you might like to see," he stepped aside to let John pass. Helen was so surprised that she almost burst into tears when she saw her oldest son. John walked across to her bed and she took his hand.

"What are you doing here?"

"Well, Ben called and told me what happened yesterday so I thought I should take a break and come and see you guys."

"You shouldn't have. I mean, I'm so happy to see you but you're so busy," she wouldn't let go of John's hand.

"Mom, there are some things that are more important than work, like you being in hospital. I had to come home to see what it is you've been up to."

"I'm fine and hopefully back home soon. How long do you plan to stay?"

"I've taken at least one week off but plan to stay for two since I can work from here if necessary. And I'm looking forward to spend some time here with you all."

Helen then remembered that Ben was there too.

"Sorry, Ben, I didn't mean to blank you out. How are things at home? Who's looking after the chickens?"

"Everything's fine, mom, and under control. Emma has taken on the responsibility of your hens apart from this evening where I'm doing them. I'll try not to forget them." He gave her a cheeky little smile.

"You better not forget them," she grabbed his hand too and smiled.

"I'm so pleased I have you both here." She kept looking from one to the other. *Seeing John had really brought out the color in her cheeks*, Ben thought. She looked so much better now which made him feel a bit better. Perhaps Emma was right that she would be fine.

"Let's hope we can get you home soon, then we can all be together at home. I have to say that you definitely look a lot better than yesterday."

"Thank you, Ben. I feel better, just very tired."

"You'll never guess who we ran into down at the café."

"Any clues? I've no idea," she looked at John.

"Well, do you remember Maria?"

"Oh yes, that lovely girl from school. You and her spent most of your free time together," she looked at Ben. "What is she doing now? Is she working here?"

"No, she works in the tourist shop in town according to the card she gave me." John showed it to Helen. "She suggested that the three of us and Emma should meet up over coffee while I'm home to have a catch-up."

"That would be nice for all of you. Nothing like a good old catch-up." Helen looked at the both of them. "And nice of her to think of Emma too. By the way, she dropped in a bit earlier today. So nice to see her."

It wasn't difficult to see how much Helen adored Emma. *That girl could practically not do anything wrong in his mother's eyes,* Ben thought. John had also noticed the way Helen spoke about Emma and more to the point how she was looking at Ben when she did it.

They carried on for a little while chatting about this and that. After an hour or so, Ben said he had to head home and do some work.

"Dad should be here soon so you can either stay and come home with him or come with me now."

Ben was looking at John, hoping that he would opt for the stay as he wanted to make a couple of calls on the way back. And he could really do with some time on his own to think it all through. There was the meeting with the Bank the next day, he needed to make sure he had all the relevant papers ready. It wouldn't be easy to do that with John in the house as he was trying to avoid telling him about it. Now leaving his brother here wasn't without danger. John could start asking questions and their parents could decide to tell him what was going on but it was a risk he had to take. All he could do was pray that they wouldn't say anything. John opted to stay and Ben gave his mother a kiss.

"I'll try and make it in tomorrow if you're not home by then."

"Good to see you, son. Love you and don't forget the chickens." Helen waved at him.

Bill entered as Ben was walking out of the room.

"Good timing, dad. I'll leave you to bring John home with you" – all four of them laughed. *It felt so good to hear that,* Ben thought. It had been a while since they as a family had done that. Strange how a relatively serious situation like this could bring happiness to them all.

{ 6 }

Back in the car Ben closed his eyes and tried to relax. He felt so tired and without thinking he dialed Emma's number. It only rang a couple of times before she answered it.

"Hi, Ben! What's up?"

Ben realized that he didn't really know why he had called her. He paused for a second.

"Hey, Emma. Just wanted to thank you for looking in on mom earlier on." Oh gosh, was that what he could come up with?

"That's okay. I thought she looked a lot better today. Are you okay?" Emma knew Ben well enough to know that there had to be more to it than that.

At the same time Ben was desperately trying to come up with something sensible to say and then he remembered Maria.

"Oh, we ran into Maria at the hospital. Do you remember her?"

"Yeah, of course I do. She runs the tourist shop in town," Emma replied.

"Well, she'd like us all to get together over coffee one day while John is home and she asked us to bring you along."

"Okay, that sounds great, Ben."

"We can sort it out tomorrow once I've had my meeting with the Bank."

Ben hadn't mentioned his brother so Emma decided to ask.

"How was it seeing John, by the way? Does your mom know he has come home to visit?"

Ben thought for a second about whether to tell her about what John had said about how his PA was like a mother to him but decided not to. Instead, he just said, "Yeah, it was okay. He's planning to stay for a couple of weeks but he also mentioned something about maybe moving back here. And yes, I did take him to see her, she was very happy to see him as you can imagine."

"Really – moving back here?"

"That's what he said. We can't say anything to mom or dad about it and I can't see it happening anyway. Well, I'll head home and get things ready for tomorrow. See you in the morning."

Ben felt a bit more relaxed now he had spoken to Emma. She somehow had a calming effect on him, he wasn't sure why.

Emma, on the other hand, was a little puzzled by Ben's call and wasn't sure what to make of it. *Going to be some interesting days ahead*, she thought.

On the way back, Ben was thinking of Maria. Funny how they hadn't seen each other for the best part of ten years and yet back when they were at school together, they spent most of their spare time together. They were practically inseparable and it made him smile thinking of it. It had never been more than a very good friendship and he had never thought of her in any other way. John had been a bit jealous of him back then as he had always had a soft spot for her but somehow Maria never really noticed him probably because she loved the outdoors like Ben.

He began to wonder why their friendship had ended or more like died out. After all, they still live in the same area. *Just one of those things that happen as you move on in life,* he thought. Well, it will be good to meet up with her again. She didn't look like she had changed a lot. His thoughts then turned to whether she had ever got married – according to the card she had given John she still had the same surname.

Once back home Ben went straight into the office and got on with the paperwork for the meeting the following day. He wasn't sure what he would need or should bring but decided that if he took all the letters that the Bank had sent, and the agreement, it should do. Then he stuffed it all in an envelope and took it down to his place, that way it was out of sight. Ben couldn't help but feel quite relieved once that was out of the way and now, he could get on with the rest of the jobs for the day. There were a couple of messages on the answering machine asking for a ride the following morning. His meeting with the bank was at 11 so there was no way he could do it but as things stood, he couldn't really turn them down either. There was no reason why Emma couldn't do it, he thought and dialed her number.

"You again," he could hear the laugh as she answered the phone.

"Yeah, I have a problem. My meeting tomorrow is at 11 but I've just had a couple of bookings for the morning as well and I can't do them both. Would you be kind enough to take the ride?" He knew she would say yes but felt that if they arranged it today, they wouldn't have to talk about it in front of anyone tomorrow morning.

"No problem! Of course, I'll do that."

"If the others ask why you and not me, we'll just say that I had planned to go and look at something. I don't want them to know about my meeting yet." Ben wanted to have a plan they both agreed to in case questions were asked.

"I'm pretty sure they won't ask but yeah, that sounds like a plan. Now enjoy your evening and try not to think about tomorrow."

"Thanks for the advice, Emma. I'll try my best. See you in the morning."

"See you and don't forget the chickens." She hung up.

Oh yeah, he had kind of forgotten about them but it was too early yet so he decided to write a note and put it on the kitchen table. That way he wouldn't forget them. Next, he went up to collect his few things from his old bedroom and headed down to his place.

There was no need for him to stay at the house tonight with John being home. His phone rang just as he got inside the door. It was John and immediately Ben started to think that something had happened to this mother.

"Everything okay?" Ben tried to sound calm.

"Yes, everything's fine but mom is concerned about what we are going to have for dinner tonight."

Ben felt a big relief followed by another panic.

"To be honest, I haven't given it a thought. I'm not a cook," he quickly replied.

"That's okay. Dad and I'll pick some pizzas on the way home if that's okay with you."

"Suits me." He could hear John laugh.

"It has to be simple as I can't cook either and we both know dad's skills when it comes to the kitchen."

"Okay. Simple sounds good to me."

"We'll leave soon so shall we say about an hour?"

"That's fine by me." Ben couldn't quite believe that John had said that. Did he really say he couldn't cook and yet he lived on his own? How did he survive?

As promised, Bill and John returned home about an hour later with a couple of pizzas they had picked up. It was okay but definitely not mother's cooking Ben thought.

"Well, we can't live on pizza every day while moms in hospital," Bill looked at them both. "We will have to come up with something." He turned to John. "Are you really going to tell me that you don't cook, son?" Bill's glasses were half way down his nose which made him look like a school teacher having a serious talk with a student.

Ben couldn't help laughing and carried on where Bill had stopped.

"What do you live on in New York?"

John felt he was being squeezed into a corner.

"Okay, okay I can do a very tiny bit but I spend most days out either at work or at various receptions. And it's so easy to grab something to eat. Why would I sit at home eating all on my own?"

"That's called family, John. Haven't you got a girlfriend?"

Bill then turned to Ben. "And you've had it easy. Perhaps it's time you two start to learn to cook," he laughed.

"Well, what about you, dad?" John was ready to fight back now.

"Oh, I'm too old now to learn new things."

"I'm sure we can work something out. Maybe we could ask Emma to help us." Ben had got up and started to tidy up after their dinner. It was fairly easy as most of it just went in the trash.

"That's a good idea, Ben." John was now helping him.

"Well, I don't know if she can cook but it's worth asking. And let's hope mom comes home soon." Ben had started to regret bringing Emma into the conversation especially when he heard Bill's next question. He quickly turned around to look at his dad but to his relief saw that he was looking at John.

"So, do you have a girlfriend?" Bill wasn't finished with quizzing John.

"Not really," John replied. "I thought I had but it turned out that she wasn't what I thought she was." He went on to tell his father about what had happened when Ben had given him the news about their mother.

"She doesn't sound too good to me. I think you can do better than that, son." Bill laughed.

"Well, enough about me. What about you, Ben? Do you have one?"

Ben nearly choked on his beer – he should have seen that question coming really.

"No, most definitely not; I'm not going there again," he

said. "I got my feelings hurt very badly once and don't wanna try that again."

Yes, that was true, even John remembered that. It was a couple of years after he had finished school and her name was Lisa. They had been dating for two years and everyone thought that Ben was taken. He had even been to look at a ring so he could propose to her. Then one day out of the blue she announced that she was moving; she wanted to see things, do some traveling and she thought it would be best if they went their separate ways. It had hit Ben very hard and he had spent a lot of time out on his horse, didn't speak to anyone and generally just kept to himself.

"Did you ever hear from Lisa again?" John asked.

"Nope, not once and that's even after she said she would keep in touch." Ben didn't really want to talk about it. Even now talking about it sent shivers down his spine.

"Well, I never really liked her," Bill added in.

"You can't let that control the rest of your life, Ben. You need to forget about it and move on." John stopped short of saying 'open your eyes to see what is in front of you' as he thought it might be pushing a bit too hard. But he was pretty sure that there was some sort of chemistry between his brother and Emma that neither of them had seen yet.

"Well, I can't see how I can trust anyone after that. How do you know it's going to work out? *You* don't seem to have found the one yet." *This is not getting any better*, Ben thought and all he could think of was escaping down to his place without being rude.

"You wait and see; it'll happen one day," John looked at

Bill. "Isn't that right, dad? How did you meet mom? I don't remember ever hearing about that."

"I remember that as clear as if it was yesterday. There was a barn dance on one of the other ranches and I went along with a friend of mine. We were stood at the bar looking around to see who was there – knew quite a few and then amongst them all was this stunning young lady. My buddy Harry dared me to go and ask her to dance. So, after I finished my drink, I went over and asked if she'd like to dance. To my surprise and joy, she said yes and I think we spent most of the evening on the dance floor together. Over the next few months, we kept meeting up at various parties. Then I asked if she'd like to join me on a ride which she enjoyed so much that it became a regular thing. After about four months, I proposed to her and she said yes. It just felt right and here we are thirty-five years later, still very much in love with each other."

Ben could see his dad getting emotional talking about it. The last days' event had hit his father hard; he had come close to lose the love of his life. After a little pause, Bill carried on. "So, sons, if I can give you one piece of advice, it would be not to let the past control what you do in the future. Especially you, Ben, as I know what happened to you hit you very hard."

Bill then turned and looked at John.

"Now, as for you: Don't forget that there's a thing called family before it's too late. Work isn't everything."

Both John and Ben didn't really know what to reply to that and before they could say anything, Bill had got up.

"Now if you'll excuse me, I'll go to bed as I didn't sleep that well last night and it's catching up with me now. I hope you don't mind, Ben, if I spend most of the day at the hospital tomorrow. Your mom should get some results and if they're okay, she might even be allowed home which would be nice. The house doesn't feel the same without her here."

"Yes, I'll be fine, dad, don't worry about me. I have Emma and also John if he is strong enough." Ben looked at John and felt relieved that the conversation had moved on. "See you tomorrow. Good night, dad." Ben had got up and was thinking of heading back to his.

"Want another beer?" John looked at Ben and headed for the kitchen to get one for himself.

Ben thought for a second and said yes but at the same time thought it might have been a bad idea. John could start asking him questions but on the other hand, there was a danger that if he left John alone, he would start looking at things.

John returned with the two beers and he had also found some potato chips which he put on the table in front of them.

"Did you and Maria ever date?"

"Nope, we were just good friends back then." Ben looked at John.

He was a bit surprised by the question. Why was he thinking of that now?

"Why you asking?"

Instead of answering the question, John went on:

"So, what's the story about Emma? Do you like her?"

"She's a good friend and she works for us. Why are you

asking me all these questions?" Ben was beginning to feel slightly uncomfortable with all these personal questions and he wanted to put a stop to it before it got out of control. "There's nothing going on between her and me, if that's what you're thinking," he hoped that would be the end of that conversation.

John smiled. He, on the other hand, wasn't convinced by Ben's answer but decided that today was not the day to dig deeper into that subject. He knew Emma was very much loved by his parents; they practically talked about her as if she was their own daughter. He also knew that it was Emma that eventually had gotten Ben through the break up with Lisa.

John took a sip of his beer.

"It was really good to see Maria today, don't you think?"

"Yeah, strange how we haven't run into each other before." Ben was glad for the change of subject.

"I'll call her tomorrow and try and arrange something, perhaps for the weekend?"

"Yeah, or perhaps Friday I think we have rides at the weekend." Ben got up and went to double check the diary but was pretty sure Friday would be good. "There are no rides booked so we can keep that day clear if that suits her."

"Okay, I'll see what we can arrange. Speaking of rides. You don't seem to be that busy at the moment. Is everything going okay here?"

"Yeah, it's fine." Ben had to use all his reserves trying to hide the shock of the question. Had John heard something or had his parents said anything to him after he left him at the hospital with them? He was panicking but managed to keep it under control, at least on the outside. His heart was going as fast as it had ever done but luckily John couldn't see that. "Just a couple of quiet days which is good with mom in hospital." He hoped John bought the story as he really didn't feel like being forced to tell him what was going on. At some point, John would work it out but if it could wait until he had seen the Bank tomorrow, he would feel better about it as he then would know exactly where they stood in terms of losing the ranch or not.

"Oh, that's some luck then." Again, John wasn't convinced that was the full story but he was too tired to keep going. It had been a long day, he had left New York very early that morning and due to the time zone difference, he had gained a couple of hours.

"Well, I'll speak to Maria tomorrow and let you know. Will probably head into town and go for a wander around after breakfast." John got up. "Think I'm going to call it a day if you don't mind. The events of the last twenty-four hours have finally caught up with me I think."

Thank God for that, Ben thought. He wasn't sure he could keep the barriers up much longer.

"No problem, I'll head down to my place and leave you in charge of looking after dad. See you tomorrow morning. Good night."

Once alone, he felt a big relief. What an evening. First, they dug up his past, a very sore one, and then John's questions. If it had gone on much longer, he wouldn't have been able to hold up the fort. His head was spinning like a propeller out of control and it had given him a headache.

On the way down to his place he couldn't help but feel irritated by the fact that they had brought up the subject of Lisa again. It had brought back painful memories. As if he didn't have enough on his plate. He couldn't help thinking what ever happened to her, where was she now and what was she doing? He had never heard from or seen her again but there was no doubt that she had hurt his feelings really badly and for that he could never forgive her.

He unlocked the door and once inside he sat down. How was he going to be able to sleep now? He remembered clearly all the sleepless nights he had back then, he would often get up and go for a walk outside in the middle of the night looking at the stars. Of all nights this was one where it was important that he got some sleep as he had a very challenging day ahead of him.

He looked at his phone and wondered if he should call Emma. She had said to contact him if he felt he needed to talk or if anything happened. Emma was the only one that had really understood his feelings and what he had gone through back then. He knew it was thanks to her that he had got through it in the end, purely by accident. He suddenly remembered John's comment earlier about Emma and his relationship with her. How could his brother even think that there was something there? Emma was Ben's closest friend, the only one he really felt he could trust and that was something completely different in Ben's mind. In the end, he decided to send her a message instead. He told her what had happened but left out John's comment. Didn't take long for a reply to come back: *Oh no. You okay? Do you want to talk?*

Before he could answer, she was calling him.

"Sorry, just thought it'd be easier if we actually talked rather than texted."

She sounded so caring on the phone, there was something about her voice that made Ben relax a little.

"Why did they have to dig her up? Don't they know how I feel about that stuff?"

"They probably didn't really think about it, after all they're men and they tend not to think about feelings. You know that. The best thing you can do is try not to think about her, remember she's history now."

"Easier said than done."

"I know but no point in wasting energy on her. You've come a long way and have some important things coming up which you can handle. Don't let her spoil it for you."

She was right about that. The question was how he was going to get her out of his mind. Definitely easier said than done. "Try and think of it this way. Imagine you get an agreement with the bank and that way you keep the ranch. What would you like to do with it? And try not to think of money here."

"But what if I don't get an agreement?"

"You don't know until tomorrow so why not try and have some sweet dreams about it tonight? You might even come up with an idea that could help you get that agreement."

They kept talking about what would be nice to do if he had all the money he needed. Ben was beginning to feel more positive about it all. In the end, he realized that it was getting late and that they probably should stop talking and get some sleep.

"Hey, we better stop, Emma. It's late. Thank you so much for listening to me."

"Yeah, you're right. Now I'm pretty sure you'll be fine tomorrow and it will all go well."

"Thank you. You're a star. Good night."

"You're welcome. Sweet dreams."

Somehow, she had done it again. He could feel his eyelids getting heavier and decided to try and get some sleep. It was going to be a difficult day tomorrow; one he wasn't looking forward to but he knew he had to get through it.

{ 7 }

Ben was sat drinking his coffee and John had just walked into the kitchen when Emma showed up at the door.

"Morning, all!" She put the basket with eggs on the table. "Nice to see you, John. It's been a while."

"Morning, Emma. Are you always so happy and cheerful early in the morning?" John was hardly awake but still managed to give her a hug. He then went to get a mug and poured himself a coffee.

"Want some coffee, Emma?"

"Yes, please. Any news on Helen?" Emma looked from John to Ben.

"Dad said last night that she'll be getting some results today and hopefully she can then be discharged either later today or tomorrow." Ben's eyes met hers, bit like he was just checking in with her.

"Anyone else for a piece of toast?" John looked at them both at the same time as Ben was looking at Emma. *Yeah, there's something there*, he thought to himself.

"No, thanks; already had breakfast." Emma sat down with her coffee next to Ben.

"What about you, Ben, would you like toast?"

"No, thanks, we better get going." He got up. Somehow John's chatting to Emma irritated him.

"What are we doing first?" Emma looked at him and at the same time tried to finish her coffee in a hurry.

"We got to check the cattle first. Think there's a couple of lame ones we might have to deal with."

He started to head for the door. Emma was puzzled; there was nothing wrong with them yesterday. This has to have something to do with his meeting later she thought.

"Okay. Be there in a second!" She turned to John. "You going in to see Helen this morning?"

"Dad is. I'll head into town and have a wander around. Anything to look out for?"

"Not really, nothing's changed I think."

"You're probably right. Oh, did Ben tell you we ran into Maria yesterday?" Emma noticed John's big smile when he mentioned her name.

"Yeah, he did."

"Why did those two never get together? They were so close back then."

"Don't know, maybe something to do with Lisa. I better be going. Nice to see you."

"Nice to see you, too. Oh, and I'll try and set up a get together with Maria. I take it Ben told you about our plan."

"Yeah, that would be great. Haven't seen her for a while." She could hear the truck starting. "Better get going. See you later, and say hello to Maria from me."

"Will do. Have fun with the old grumpy man."

She hasn't really changed, John thought as he watched her getting in the truck. *Still the happy girl I remember.* And she seems to have a way of handling Ben. What a shame he can't see it. John hadn't noticed that Bill had come down and was right behind him.

"What you looking at, son?"

"Oh, didn't hear you coming, dad. Morning. I was just watching Emma and Ben drive off to see the cattle. They're a perfect couple, don't you think?"

"Well, that's what your mom keeps saying but Ben doesn't seem to be interested in her in that way."

"He'll get there one day," said John even if it meant that he had to give him a push in that direction.

"Let's just hope it won't be too late by then," Bill sat down with his coffee.

Ben couldn't put his finger on why he found it irritating that John was chatting to Emma, he just did.

"Sorry, I just had to finish my coffee," Emma jumped in the truck. Ben put the truck in gear and they headed up the road. They drove for a little while in silence. Emma could see that Ben was very tense and he had that same look on his face which he had in the kitchen.

"So, how many do you think are lame?" She knew that she had to try and get him talking. It wouldn't be in his favor to be in this frame of mind when he was going to the meeting later.

"I don't know, we'll have to see when we get there."

She knew for a fact that there was no sign of lame cattle yesterday and he was just using it as a cover up for something else. *Time to get things straight,* she thought.

"Ben, we were both up there yesterday and there was

nothing wrong then. This isn't about lame cattle, is it?" She looked at him.

"Maybe not." Ben kept looking straight ahead. He should have known that she could read him like a book. Why did he ever think that he could hide things from her?

"What else did you talk about last night?" Emma was pretty sure this had something to do with last night's chat between Bill, John and Ben. "Have they found out about the meeting?"

"Nope," was all Ben said.

They had reached the field and Emma got out to open the gate. Once the truck was in the field and the gate closed, Ben decided to drive straight down to his favorite spot. He got out and went to sit down at his favorite spot. Emma followed him. Yes, this had definitely nothing to do with the cattle as they had only glanced at them as they drove past them on the way to the river.

"So, what did you talk about then?" She sat down next to him trying to work out what had happened last night. She knew about Lisa but they had talked that through last night. There had to be more to the story. She was pretty sure this wasn't just worry about the meeting with the bank; there seemed to be a small amount of anger building up.

Ben kept staring out over the river and after a little while he finally started to talk.

"John thought we were more than just friends."

"Oh." That was not what she had expected to come up. It hadn't even crossed her mind. Yes, she liked Ben a lot but for it to be more than just friendship, well, she hadn't thought of it that way.

"Why did he ask you that?" She knew that there had to be more and at the same time she was busy trying to get clear on what she thought of the subject.

"Well, dad started asking John about his life in New York and his girlfriends. Then after a while, John decided it was my turn to be grilled. And that was when they brought up Lisa. I told them that I was not going there again, that I'd never let myself go through that pain again."

"Okay."

"I said we were just very good friends and then he starts chatting you up this morning."

John chatting her up. Was that what he thought was happening this morning? And why would that bother him if he wasn't 'going there again' as he had put it? Well, now we are getting somewhere, she thought.

"Ben, I haven't seen John in a long time. Trust me it was just two good friends meeting again and no more than that."

She didn't really know what else to say to that. She had never really had any feelings for John; he was just a good friend. She looked at Ben and a strange or different feeling came over her. She had to stop it and concentrate on helping Ben, she was his friend and he needed her right now.

"Trust me, Ben. There's nothing going on between me and John and there never will be."

Ben turned to look at her, he couldn't help but feel relieved to hear that but on the other hand, sad. Why should he be the one holding her back from finding her love just because it hadn't worked out for him? And there she was again. Why couldn't he get her out of his head?

"Ben, there's something I'd like to tell you, something I heard a couple of weeks ago but I didn't want to say anything back then." Emma thought for a second of their conversation last night and decided that she wouldn't keep secrets from him. She had never liked Lisa. "I ran into an old school friend who told me something about Lisa. And now that she's been mentioned I feel that I should tell you this as I don't like to keep secrets from you. And maybe this latest info will help you move on."

"What is it?" He stared at her.

"She's now living in LA and on to her second marriage already."

"Really?" Ben shook his head. It didn't really surprise him at all. Then he turned to face her.

"I don't understand why she can still mess with my head?"

"That's because she really hurt your feelings back then. When it comes to trust and commitment, you are a very sensitive guy. You're better off without her and one day you'll find someone who will love you for who and what you are."

"Think so?" He looked at her with a little smile and thought if he could find a girl just like Emma, he might be able to open his heart again.

"Yeah, you're not that bad looking too," she laughed and got up. "Hey, think we better get on with it. Don't forget you have a meeting to get to." She jumped in the truck and Ben followed.

Before he turned the key, he looked at her.

"Thank you for this. You were right; it did help getting it out."

They did a quick tour around the cattle which all seemed fine and then headed home. By the time they got back to the ranch both Bill and John had gone. This suited Ben as he could get ready for the meeting and Emma could take the ride without anyone asking questions.

On the way in to town he called in at the yard just to check that Emma had it all under control.

"We'll be fine," Emma gave him a big smile. "Good luck with your meeting. I'm sure we can sort this out." She then turned her attention to the horses and the customers who had arrived.

Ben quickly got in his truck and headed to town. What would he do without her? Not only was she a very capable girl when it came to horses but she was also a very good listener.

As he got closer to the Bank, Ben started to look for somewhere to park his truck. There was one just across the street from the bank. *Perfect*, he thought as he turned the engine off, took a couple of deep breaths, got out and headed across the street towards the Bank.

Once inside he went straight across the room to the lady at the help desk and announced he was there. She told him to sit down and that someone would be with him shortly. His heart was racing and he found it difficult to sit still. Would he walk out of here with a deal? And how long would it take? He had no idea. As he was sat there looking around, he felt like all the staff were watching him as he was the only customer in there. He could feel his hands getting tight – the letter in his hands was being squeezed.

Yeah, the letter that stated that they had until the end of the month which was only a few weeks away to pay off the outstanding part of the mortgage. Somehow, he was hoping that they would take their situation into consideration and extend it for a bit which still left him with a problem but gave him time. The fact that he had only just discovered the problem and that his mom had been taken ill. Surely that would be the best for all parties, he thought but he also knew about the Bank, or more like the manager, Mr. Miles's reputation. He was known for not being too kind and helpful to those who didn't stick to their agreement. What would happen to him and his parents if he failed today and what about Emma?

Finally, after what felt like hours, he heard someone say:

"Hello, Mr. Jackson. And how are you today?"

Mr. Miles was stood in front of Ben with a big smile. How could he not have noticed him coming? And how can a man look so happy knowing that he is about to destroy a family's life? He got up and reached out to shake Mr. Miles's hand. What kind of hand shake do you call that apart from being a very sweaty one? Ben had already taken a big dislike to him.

"Come on in," Mr. Miles walked ahead of him. Ben could feel his legs turn into jelly. *Now this is it*, he thought. *Pull yourself together, man, and show him that he can't just walk all over you.*

Ben was finally out in the fresh air. He had a massive headache but felt he had achieved a little. The Bank had after lengthy discussion agreed to give him an extra month, not that it was going to help him a lot, he thought, but at least he had a bit more time on his hands. He looked both ways and headed across the street to his truck. Just as he was about to get in it, he heard someone calling.

"Hey, Ben! What are you doing here?"

Damn, he had been spotted; it was John and Maria. He had been so focused on his meeting that he had failed to see that he had in fact parked right outside the tourist shop.

"What were you doing over there?" John looked straight at him. Well, Ben couldn't really lie to them as they had seen him come from the Bank. "Is everything okay?" John kept looking at him very directly.

Ben took a deep breath, he had to tell his brother now and it was probably for the best anyway. "No, it isn't."

Maria who had been very close friends with Ben all those years ago could see that Ben was not in the best way.

"Hey, come in here. I don't think this is a discussion for a street audience." She grabbed Ben's hand and took them into a small room at the back of the shop where there were a few chairs and a small table.

"Tea or coffee?" She looked at them both.

"Coffee would be good. Thanks, Maria." Ben felt relieved that they were out of sight now as he wasn't sure if he could hold it all together much longer. He sank into a chair like he had been caught doing something he shouldn't have done.

"You better tell me what's going on now. I had a feeling last night that you were hiding something." John sat down across from his brother. Maria returned with three cups of coffee and some cookies.

"Thought we could use some of these right now," she managed to squeeze it all on to the table.

Ben looked at them both. Should he really be telling John about their finances in front of Maria? John could see his thinking.

"Maria is a very good friend we just haven't seen in a long time and I'm pretty sure that she will be helpful to us. So, tell us what's going on."

Ben started to tell them about the letter and the state of affairs and how he had only just found out.

"I never knew that there was a mortgage. What was it for?"

Part of Ben was surprised by John not knowing about it and part of him knew his parents wouldn't have told him. Ben explained about the storm and the damaged roof and buildings.

"I see. Why haven't I heard about this?"

"To be honest, I didn't know anything about the financial situation either, it has never been talked about. I did ask the other day, when I saw the letter, if everything was okay. I was told that it was nothing to worry about." Ben kept fiddling with his cup, staring into it. He didn't dare to look up. "I know it's my fault but since dad stopped doing any of the physical work it kind of made sense that they dealt with the admin part of it while I did the outside."

"No, Ben, this is not your fault." Maria broke in now. She sat down next to him and put her arm around his shoulders.

"I've known you for a long time. I might not have seen a lot of you over the last few years but back in the day you were a hard worker and I will put money on that you still are. I also know how hard it is to hand things on. Just look at this place. It belongs to my aunt and uncle; they're both seventy now. It could do with a facelift but they're reluctant to let me do it."

"I agree with Maria. This is not your fault, Ben." John suddenly realized how difficult a situation Ben was in not only financially but also in terms of running a business with their parents. "Now we need to have a look at this and try and put a plan together. I take it that you told Emma about all this?"

Ben nodded. "Yeah, unfortunately she can read me like a book." He stopped short of telling them about Emma overhearing his parents arguing whether to tell him or not about the letters.

"There's absolutely nothing wrong with that, brother."

"Well, John, our plan seems to be perfectly timed." Maria looked at Ben. "Just before we spotted you, we agreed to have our coffee get-together on Friday morning. Why don't we all have a think about what we could do to try and save the ranch and then we can talk about it on Friday?"

"Good plan, Maria," John looked at her smiling.

"Eh, why do you want to get involved in this mess?" Ben was confused but also worried about too many people knowing about it. He hadn't told his parents yet. What would they say?

Maria looked at them both, took a deep breath and said,

"We used to be very good friends, Ben, and just because

we haven't been in touch with each other, doesn't mean we are not still friends. I'd love to help you if I can. I may not have heaps of money or a rich uncle but I do know a thing or two about advertising. Remember I run a tourist shop here. There must be something we can do to turn the business around. Your rides used to be so popular."

"That would be great," John replied before Ben could say anything. "Friday, 11 am, here. That's a deal then. Thank you, Maria, for doing this."

Ben's head was spinning. What just happened here? He felt relieved that he wasn't the only one that knew about the problem now but at the same time a bit concerned.

"Maria, this is very kind of you but can I ask you one big favor? Please don't tell anyone about it. I haven't told mom and dad what I know and with mom in the hospital, you know..."

"Won't say a word, buddy. Well, I better get back to work. See you both on Friday! Looking forward to it."

Both Ben and John got up and Maria gave each of them a big hug. She then looked Ben straight in the eyes.

"Look, it'll work out okay, my friend."

Ben was lost for words; he had forgotten how kind she was. "Thanks, Maria." It was all he could manage to say. He headed out of the shop with John following behind.

What to do next? Should he go home or should he go and see his parents at the hospital? John could see his brother was looking lost and went to put his hands on Ben's shoulders.

"I know I haven't been home a lot but I promise you that I'll do my best to help you while I'm here."

"Thanks, brother. What do I do now? Should I tell mom and dad?"

"I think you need to tell them soon especially with mom in hospital."

"What do I say?" Ben glanced across the street.

"Say it as it is. If you like, I'll come with you. Sooner or later, they'll have realized that if the business is going to carry on, you'll have to be in on the details. I think I know you well enough to say that if anyone can carry this one and make it work, it will be you."

Ben couldn't quite believe what John had just said. Did he really mean that he was capable of doing this? Well, he might as well get it over with now and as John had offered to come with him it would make it easier. That way his parents couldn't just brush him away like they had done up to now.

"Well, we better head over there now and get it over with then," he looked at John. "Just to be clear, I am happy for you helping me but I don't want you to bail us out. I have to come up with something that both the bank and I or we can agree on. Okay?"

"Yes, I hear you, brother – I am not sure how much we are talking about in terms of dollars, but just so you know if it comes to it, I can help you financially. I know you don't want it but, as a last resort."

"Yeah, but it will be as a last resort." Ben had no intention to borrow money off John if he could avoid it. He didn't want to be in debt to him or worse having him coming home to run it together with him. He wanted to be able to run the ranch his way. The other thing was, how long did John plan to stay? Was he just going to come up with fancy ideas and then disappear again? He had a habit of not hanging around for too long.

"I'm parked just around the corner so I'll follow you to the hospital." John had got his keys out and started to head for his car.

"Alright, see you there." He had to stop thinking of what John might or might not do. Right now, he had offered to come with him and support him as he was going to tell their parents about it all. And for that Ben was truly grateful.

{ 8 }

As they walked in through the doors of the hospital, Ben could feel his stomach turn, his hands were getting all restless and he felt he couldn't breathe. He was wondering how they would take the news. John had agreed to that it was Ben that would be telling them the news. After all, it was Ben that had discovered the problem and also Ben that had got the Bank to give them an extra month. John was only there to support him. It was not going to be easy by any means but it had to be done. One thing was to tell them, another was how they were going to move forward in terms of trying to save the ranch. As they approached their mother's room, the doctor came out.

"Morning, or is it afternoon now?" he looked at his watch. "She's all set to be discharged later."

Oh boy, that was good news. Ben looked at John.

"Shouldn't we wait till she gets home, John?"

"No, you're better off getting it done now; waiting will only drag it out. Now come on and remember I got your back. You're not on your own." John opened the door and Ben walked in.

Helen was sat up in bed looking so much better.

"You've come just at the right time. I'll be coming home this afternoon but under strong advice to take it easy and avoid stress."

She looked so happy, and now I am going to spoil it all, Ben thought. He turned to look at John as if to say 'let's wait' but John just nodded and with his arm gave Ben a little push. Ben could feel his stomach tying itself in knots.

Helen began to look concerned. Before Ben had a chance to say anything, Helen broke the silence. "What's up Ben? You look like you've seen a ghost."

"Don't know about a ghost but yes, I have some news." He went on to explain how he had seen the letter and had the meeting with the Bank earlier. "Why didn't you want to tell me about this?" He looked at his parents. Holding each other's hand, they sat very quietly for a moment.

"We didn't want to burden you with it, we hoped that we could get it sorted. Sorry, Ben, we should have told you." Helen reached out to take Ben's hand. "When it first started, we were hoping that things would improve but they didn't, now we've let you down or failed you by losing it all." Bill was looking down and shaking his head.

"We are very sorry, son."

"Nothing is lost yet," it was John's turn to say something. "I am not sure why you didn't speak to me either as I work in the money world but that's a different matter. Ben and I will have a look through it all and try to come up with a plan. The good news is that Ben has managed to get a bit longer with the Bank, which will give us time to try and put a plan together."

John and Ben looked at each other. However desperately Ben wanted to do this on his own, he realized it would be silly not to take advantage of his brother's help but as long as it could be on his terms. He had to make sure of that. He looked at his parents.

"We will try our best to save the ranch. Mom, I'm glad you'll be coming home but for now John and I will take on the books if you don't mind. The doctor has just told us that you have to rest. We'll allow you to supervise us in the kitchen." Ben said that last bit with a smile. "I better get back and do some work now. I'll see you later at home." He gave his mom a kiss before he left.

John followed him out of the room.

"Well done, brother. At least they know now and I promise you that I'll help you save Jackson Ranch. Now, are you happy for me to stay a bit longer just to make sure they're okay or do you need me at home?"

"Thanks, John. No, I'll be okay, I have Emma to help. See you back home." Ben headed for the exit.

Once in the truck he sat for a while trying to let it all sink in. It had been a couple of pretty tough hours. His world had been turned upside down and the future not looking good but at least he had managed to get an extension from the Bank. What was he going to do – he put his head in his hand. His phone vibrated – a message had come through – eventually he looked at it, it was from Emma. She had done the ride and was wondering if he wanted anything else done. Right, he had to get back and take control. He thought of texting her back but decided to give her a call instead.

"How did it go with the Bank?" Ben was a bit surprised how quick she answered but then realized that the outcome would affect her too.

"Well, I'm still alive. They've given me an extension due to the circumstances."

"That's good news."

"Yeah. And I ran into John and Maria as I left the bank so they know about it too."

"How did you do that? How did John react?"

"Well, it turned out that I parked right outside Maria's shop. John had absolutely no idea about the whole thing. He had a feeling that something was up but not what."

"Well, at least he knows now."

"Yeah, he came with me to the hospital as he thought it'd be best if we told mom and dad about it as well."

"I think that was very sensible. How did they take it?"

"I'll tell you when I get back. Leaving the hospital now. John's going to stay for a while to make sure they're okay."

"Okay, see you soon."

Ben found Emma in the kitchen.

"I thought I'd clean up a bit – looks like you all just left this morning," she was smiling as she took a look at Ben. "Gosh, you look like you're ready for bed. Had any lunch?" She kind of knew the answer and decided to make him a sandwich anyway.

"Nope, and yeah, I'm feeling pretty beaten up." He looked at her and thought that what he could really do with was a big hug from his best friend but managed to stop himself from seeking it. He pulled a chair out and sat down. "Oh, thanks for cleaning up. I don't think we're very domesticated or we're just used to mom doing it all. By the way, she's coming home later today."

"That's great news, Ben!" She said and put the sandwich in front of him. She pulled out a chair next to him and sat down.

"But she's gotta rest and she is not allowed to get stressed. Do you wanna join us for dinner tonight?" The last bit came out before Ben had had a chance to think about it or even speak to his brother about it. But somehow it felt as the right thing to do. Helen was very fond of Emma and then there was the whole making dinner thing as well. "One catch: you'll have to help us make dinner."

"I'd love to!"

"Great but I have no idea what we're having," he smiled. Emma laughed.

"I'm sure we can work something out."

"I better just have a quick word with John and see what he thinks." Ben dialed his brother's number.

John answered straight away and Ben filled him in on what he had just done.

"Great idea, Ben. Why don't you and Emma try and work out what we're eating and then let me know. I can do some shopping on the way home."

"Will do. Hey, don't tell mom and dad. I want it to be a surprise for them."

John agreed.

It was mid-afternoon and they decided that steak, potatoes and veggies was an easy and fairly simple option. Emma quickly checked to see what they needed and she also added a few other things on the list that she thought they would need; she was thinking of breakfast. Ben sent the list to John.

"So, tell me about your meeting," Emma thought it was about time that Ben told her about the day's event now that they had sorted dinner out.

"What?" Ben looked at Emma and suddenly realized what she was on about. He had been so tired and busy sorting the dinner out that he had forgotten to tell her what agreement he had come to with the Bank.

"They gave us a little extra time, not that I can see how that's going to help us as they still insist on us paying all the outstanding bits of the mortgage; it'll only prolong the final result. We'll lose the ranch."

"Come on, Ben, you can't think like that. How did your parents take it?"

He told her how they had reacted and that it turned out that John didn't know about the mortgage.

"Now they feel guilty that we will lose everything." Ben didn't know where to look. It was beginning to sink in that that was the most likely outcome of it. He was struggling to hold it together now but wouldn't and couldn't let himself break down in front of Emma, even though she was his best or only friend. Emma grabbed his hand.

"Ben, come on. You can save this place; *we* can save this place. There has to be a way; don't give up. Remember you're not alone; I'm here and John's here too."

"I know but I can't accept money from John. If I have to save this, it has to be on my terms. Do you understand what I mean?"

"Yeah, I think so and you will do it."

"But how are we going to raise the money that quickly?"

"I'm not sure but we'll find a way and you have to believe in that." She was sat right next to him looking very firmly at him. *Those eyes* he thought and somehow, he found it difficult to look away.

"Now, what was this about John and Maria? Why was he at her place?" Emma couldn't help thinking of the conversation she had had earlier with John.

"Oh, they were planning our little reunion. Is Friday still okay with you?"

"Well, you're the boss so I'll have to ask if I can get time off." She laughed and gave him a gentle punch.

"Hey, watch it." And for the first time in a while Ben felt a little relaxed and he could even laugh a little.

"Well, we better get on with this dinner."

Emma looked at her watch.

"It's still kind of early. Why don't we get the jobs done outside and then cook? By that time, John will be home with the groceries too."

"Good plan. Let's go." Ben needed to get some fresh air; standing too close to Emma for too long didn't do him any good. He could feel he was losing his grip and right now he had more than enough on his plate. As long as he kept his distance, he could handle it.

John returned with the groceries they had asked for and after finishing all the outside jobs, they all entered the kitchen. None of them had done a lot of cooking but Emma knew most so she made the plan of who was doing what and when. The phone rang halfway through the cooking. Ben went in to answer it and then went very quiet. John looked at him and saw his face go pale. He quickly grabbed the phone.

"Hello." It was Bill on the other end. Helen had had another blackout so she wasn't coming home today.

"Okay, keep us updated, dad." He put the phone down and turned to Emma and Ben. "Mom's not coming home today, she had a minor setback and they want to run some more tests." Ben was staring at the floor.

"I shouldn't have told them; it's my fault. Why did you let me do it?" He looked at John and could feel the anger building.

"It isn't your fault, Ben, and besides, remember I said she was in the best place. She's gonna be fine, it'll just be a couple more days."

"It is still my fault," Ben got up and headed for the door, said he was going out to get some fresh air. John was going to follow his brother but Emma stopped him.

"Just leave him. Come and help me get dinner finished, we still gotta have something to eat and we can't let it go to waste. Did Bill say anything about him coming home?"

"Yeah, he'll be back later. Why can't Ben see that it isn't his fault?"

"Not sure but I think with all the things that have happened and been mentioned, these last couple of days have stirred his dark side. He'll get there; just give him some space."

"I understand that. Believe me, it was a bit of a shock for me too. I had no idea of the financial issue here. And I'm the money expert in the family."

"Your mom always talks about how busy you are and that's why you can't come home. So, they probably didn't want to burden you with their problems."

"I know I haven't been very good at visiting but that will change now. I spoke to Ben about possibly moving back here."

"Oh, that would be good but will you be able to work here?"

"Yeah, I'll work something out but hey, please don't say anything to mom and dad as nothing is fixed yet."

"Won't say a word."

Dinner was ready but Ben had still not come back in. John was getting concerned about him.

"Where can he be? Should I go and find him?"

"I have an idea where he could be; let me go and get him." Emma was pretty sure that Ben would be around the back of the barn where you could see the sun setting behind the mountains. It was a place where he often would sit when he needed to be alone. Sure enough, there he was sat on an old tree trunk. He didn't notice her coming until she sat next to him.

"What you thinking of?" She could see he had been crying which was probably a good thing.

Ben quickly tried to wipe away the tears. He felt so embarrassed and all he could mutter was "hey".

It's about time he would let go off some of his emotions, Emma thought and put a hand on his shoulder.

"It's okay to cry, Ben. I promise you; I won't tell anyone." They sat for a bit and just watched the sunset. "It's such a beautiful view from here, I can see why you like it." Emma had never really sat down and watched the sunset from this spot before but she could see why Ben loved this spot.

He looked at her and said, "I'm scared."

"That's okay; we all get scared from time to time. What is it that you're scared of?" Emma had put her arm around his back as if to say 'you will be okay, I am here'.

"She could have died."

"But she didn't."

"I know but what if she had, it would have been my fault."

"No, Ben, it wouldn't. Remember they already knew the situation with the ranch. By telling them what you knew and that you will take care of it, you have taken some of the pressure off them."

"I know but still. What could I have done differently?"

"Nothing because you didn't know about it. Remember that. And now you have John here. He's just as shocked as you are but he's willing to help you if you will let him."

"He won't stay for long."

"Well, I'm not so sure about that. Anyway, let's go and eat. After all the cooking we did, it'd be a shame to let it go to waste, don't you think?" She got up and reached out for his hand in a gesture to him to get up and come with her. She was right again, he thought, it would be a waste to throw out the dinner. "Come, let's go, your brother is worried about you."

"Really?" he stopped and Emma looked at him.

"Come on, let's go."

"Emma," he looked at her and couldn't resist any longer.

He put his arms around her and hugged her tight. "Thank you," he whispered.

Emma was very surprised by his reaction as he never really liked being too close to others, especially women.

"You're welcome. That's what friends are for."

John was so pleased to see Ben back in and he walked over to give him a hug.

"Hey, brother, it'll all be sorted out and mom will be okay."

"Yeah, I hope so."

"And I promise you, I'll stay and help you get this place back on track."

"Thanks, brother, but I'd rather do this my way."

"Don't be silly. I can promise you that I have no intention to take this away from you. It has always been the idea that you would carry it on and that is not changing but don't forget I have contacts that might be able to help you. Okay?"

"Okay." Ben wasn't in a state to fight his brother right now and let's face it he was probably right about the help part. *I just got to be careful it doesn't get out of my control*, he thought to himself.

"Let's see how good our cooking has been. I'm starving now," Emma pulled out a chair and sat down.

"Anyone for a beer?" John looked at them both. Ben nodded but Emma declined.

"I better not, gotta drive home in a minute."

They ate in silence. In the end, Emma put her fork down.

"Well, I'd say we've passed. That was very nice. Thank you, guys." She raised her glass to both of them.

"Well, not bad for a first attempt I'd say. What do you think, Ben?" John looked at his brother.

"Can you cook every evening, Emma?" Ben looked at her with a smile.

"This wasn't just me; it was a team effort, Ben," she gave him a light push on his arm. "And it's good to see you smile. So, what time is coffee on Friday? And where are we meeting?"

"11 o'clock at the tourist shop. Maria has a little room at the back we can sit in. I'll get some things to go with the coffee as I take it you two will have things to do here first," John sounded very excited about the meeting, Ben thought and turned to Emma.

"We can drive in together if you like."

"That would make sense. I'm really looking forward to this. I haven't spoken to Maria for a while, it'll be good to catch up."

"Maria suggested that all try and have a think of what we could do to get this place back on track." John looked at them both. "And she offered to help as well."

"That's very good! She is very skilled at advertising. Well, I better head home. I'll see you guys tomorrow. Thanks for a lovely dinner even though your parents couldn't be here. At least we know what we can cook for them," she laughed as she got up and went to get her keys.

"You're welcome and thanks for the help!" said John.

As she walked out, she put a hand on Ben's shoulder.

"Okay, see you in the morning?"

"Yeah, I'll be here." He gave her a smile.

This is so painful to watch, John thought. *They are so right for each other, if only Ben could see that.* In some ways he was a bit jealous. There had been many girlfriends over the years but none of them had been that serious. He was still searching for the right one. And here was his brother with the right one in front of him without realizing it or allowing himself to see it. John decided that he had to find a way to make it happen but at the same time he knew far too well that pushing Ben too hard could end up with the wrong result.

They sat for a bit before Ben got up.

"I think I'll turn in for the day if you don't mind. Been quite a day for me."

"No problem. Just one thing. I know that you're not keen on my help and I can fully understand your reservation but I wanna help you. I have the money and I'm prepared to pay the outstanding amount if it comes to it. I also know that you won't let me but please think about it as a last resort."

"Thanks for the offer but I can't take your money. I want this place to carry on but I don't need more debt." Ben was too tired to argue with John. "But I'll let you help me on one condition. Whatever we do, I have to be happy with it. Deal?"

"Yes, I wouldn't do it any other way, Ben. Believe it or not, I do actually care about you. Now get some sleep and we can start on a fresh note tomorrow. Okay?"

"Deal – hey did you really mean that you care about me?"

"Of course, I do. You're my brother."

"Good night. See you bright and early tomorrow." Ben walked out and headed down to his place.

Once the door had closed behind him, Ben could finally relax. *What a day it had been*, he thought. It felt like he had been dragged behind a horse for miles. And how embarrassing that Emma had caught him crying; well, it would have been worse if it had been his brother. There is something special about Emma but he couldn't work out what it was.

He couldn't help thinking if it was his fault that his mother had another setback. Had it really been the right thing to tell them about his discovery? Was that why it had happened?

Then, there was John offering to help. He couldn't and wouldn't accept his brother's money, that's for sure and he was a little skeptical about his motives for helping him save the ranch. *There had to be something behind it*, he thought. Why would John be willing to lend him money; what was in it for him? And then there was Maria. Well, he hadn't seen her in years which was strange as they used to be very close. John had seemed very friendly with her and he wondered what his brother was up to there. *Surely, he would have girls in New York* he thought. *Right, that's it. I need some sleep.* He dragged himself into bed.

{ 9 }

The following day went without any problems and Helen returned home late afternoon. Ben, John and Emma prepared the same dinner as the night before, only this time it was quicker as they all knew what to do.

"Hey guys, this is kind of fun doing it together, don't you think?" Emma was busy preparing the salad.

"Well, I don't know. I'd prefer to be outside but as a one-time thing, yeah it's been fun," Ben looked at her whilst busy doing the potatoes.

"Next time, someone else can do these," he flicked the water on his fingers towards Emma.

"Watch it, pal," she said but couldn't really flick back as her hands were dry.

"I don't mind doing the steak, think this suits me," John joined in.

The phone went and Ben immediately dropped everything and ran to answer it. Thoughts were running through his head and he felt like it took forever to get to the phone. His hands were shaking. *Not again,* he thought. Emma and John watched him as he picked up the phone.

"Hello, Jackson Ranch." There was a pause for a second. Emma and John looked at each other and then back to Ben.

"Oh yeah, we can do that, no problem. So, Saturday morning, how many? Nine. Yeah, that'll be fine. We'll see you at eleven." The smile on Ben's face as he returned said it all. "Looks like we have work on Saturday," he looked at Emma and then turned to John. "Hey, why don't you join us on this group; we could use an extra pair of hands."

"Me? I haven't ridden in years," John looked at Ben.

"And? You were pretty good at it once."

"Why would you want me to come along?"

"Well, if you're going to help me rescue this place, don't you ought to know what goes on?"

"Good point, brother, but not sure what I can help with."

"Well, it's two families, so three adults and six kids ranging from six to fifteen years old. An extra pair of eyes would be good."

"That could be fun. I'll find you the perfect horse," Emma smiled and thought that would be an excellent way for John to see what they did.

"Okay, I'll do it but please be gentle with me."

"We will. Now we better get this finished. Mom and dad will be home soon." Emma couldn't help noticing Ben sounding a lot happier.

Once he had finished the potatoes, Ben went to write it all in the diary. As he made a note of the numbers, he couldn't help but smile. When did he and John last ride out together; they use to do it a lot when they were younger. John was what you would call a natural rider and Ben was pretty sure that once he was out there, he would enjoy it. Also, if his brother was serious about helping to rescue the ranch, it would be good for him to experience the jobs that was involved in running it. One other thing was that out there on horseback he would be in charge and John would have to listen to him.

A car pulled up outside the house. John called.

"Ben, they're home!"

"Okay, coming."

Helen was so surprised to see that they had actually cooked dinner for her. Bill had had to work very hard to keep it as a surprise, he had to come up with all sorts of excuses for why they didn't need to get anything before heading home.

"You didn't have to do all this." She looked at them all. "Good thing you were here, Emma. Don't think the boys could have done it without you."

"They did much better than you think, Helen." Emma gave her a hug. "Good to see you home."

And for the first time in a long time, they all sat down for dinner together.

"Thank you so much for a lovely dinner. It was very tasty I have to say." Helen looked around at them all. "I'm so glad to be back home and look forward to a night's sleep without any bells, nurses or lights to disturb me." She was feeling very tired and was longing to go to bed. "If you don't mind, I'll head off to bed now." Helen got up and started to clear the table.

"No, mom, we're doing that. Remember you have to rest." John looked at her firmly. "And we'll sort out breakfast tomorrow. Okay?"

"Well, if you insist," she put the plate down again.

"John's right, Helen. You have to follow doctor's orders. I'll continue looking after the hens, don't you worry about them.

Now I need to head home. Good night, everyone. See you in the morning!" Emma headed for the door and Ben followed her out. Once outside, he thanked her again for her help.

"You know I am happy to help," she looked at him. "Now make sure you get a good night's sleep so you can be fresh and full of ideas for our coffee meeting. I'm so looking forward to it!"

"Will try. See you in the morning." Ben watched her drive off. He found it amazing how she was always so positive. How did she do that? And of course, she was right; he had to make sure he got some sleep so he could be fresh for the events of the following day.

As he got back inside, Helen looked at him. "I hear that you are meeting over coffee tomorrow. That'll be fun."

Ben looked at John; he thought that they had agreed to keep the meeting a secret from their parents.

"Yeah, I told mom and dad that we're meeting up with Maria for coffee tomorrow so we can catch up on old times."

"Oh yeah, that's right. So much has been happening this week I've lost track of what day of the week it is," he hoped he had got away with it.

"I think it's wonderful. You used to be such good friends back in your school days."

"I am looking forward to it. Now to some more serious matters," John looked very firm and Ben wasn't sure what he was about to say. "You know that we know about the state of affairs here. You know Ben has been to see the Bank and got a small extension. We want you to know that we're going to do our best to come up with a solution that will please the

Bank and save this place. This will mean that we will need access to all documents. And on top of that we don't want you two to worry about it. Okay?"

"I promise you; I'll do my absolute best to save the ranch and now that I have John to help me, I will hopefully be able to come up with something."

Helen and Bill looked at each other, then Bill cleared his throat and said, "We are very proud of both of you boys and Ben, we have failed you for not letting you in on the situation and for that we are very sorry."

"Dad, you haven't failed me and I will make it work," Ben grabbed his father's hand. He could see the tears in his eyes.

"I know, son. We will try to support you and John as much as we can and if you succeed, this will all be yours, Ben. You've earned it as you have worked very hard and never complained."

"Thanks, dad," it was now Ben's turn to feel his eyes filling up. John came over and put a hand on his shoulder.

"Dad's right; you have earned this, brother, and trust me, we will find a solution to this."

"Oh, boys, come here. We love you both very much," Helen put her arms around both of them.

What an evening, Ben thought as he was heading down to his place. John had come along; his excuse was that he needed some fresh air but he really wanted to make sure Ben was okay. It had been quite an evening with some rather big news for him.

"Are you okay with all that?" He looked at Ben.

"Yeah, don't think it has quite sunken in yet."

"I know but I have to say I'm happy they made the decision to hand it on to you. Now we just need to get it back on track."

"But are *you* okay with it?" Ben just realized that he had been handed the ranch and John got nothing.

"Yeah, I have no problems with that. I have no idea how to run this place. It would be like putting you in charge of some of my clients in New York," he laughed. "And it will be even better when I know that you've saved it and I'll help you do that."

They had reached Ben's house.

"Want a beer, brother?" Ben looked at John.

"Thought you'd never ask."

They spent the next couple of hours talking about what Ben did on the ranch, what he would like to or think he could do, and what other ranches did. John needed to have an idea of what modern ranching was like in order to see what opportunities there were.

After John left, Ben spent some time pondering over what his father had said. He couldn't quite decide if he was angry, sad or happy. Angry with them because they hadn't told him earlier about the problems. If they had, the ranch might not have been in the situation that it was in. Sad because his parents felt they had to give it up; after all, they had worked hard all their life. Or happy as he had basically been handed the control of the ranch. What would he have done differently if he had known about it earlier? Good question and to which he had no answer right now. And if he was honest, he had no idea what to do to save it either. So, all very good handing him the reins to the ranch but what could he do? All he could hope for was that together with John, Emma and Maria they could come up with something that might just work. It was past midnight and time to get some rest. He wandered into bed.

Ben felt like he had only just gone to bed when the alarm went off. He hit snooze; he felt so tired. What was it Emma had said to him last night just before leaving? *Make sure you get some sleep so you are fresh for tomorrow.* Somehow, he had to find a way of surviving the day but right now he felt like he could turn over and sleep the rest of the day. The alarm sounded again. *Okay, okay I'll get up.* He went and threw cold water on his face and got dressed. Then he headed up to the house. What he needed was some coffee. That would get him going but it didn't look like there was anyone up; in fact, there wasn't. This surprised him a bit. He had kind of expected his mother to have coffee ready for him. Well, he thought and smiled, she is taking the doctor's orders seriously. Only one thing to do, he had to make the coffee himself. Emma arrived just as it was ready.

"You know how to time things," he said, trying to sound funny.

"Morning to you, too," she said and put the basket with eggs on the table. "Is she not up yet?" Emma put her head around the corner into the living room.

"Nope. I had to do this myself," he smiled, gesturing at the coffee. "Actually, I'm very proud of her. Looks like she's listening to doctor's orders."

"Good. So, what's the plan for the day, cowboy?"

"Think we'll head out and get things done early so we're ready. Let's take a ride up to the cattle."

"Okay." She wondered what was on his mind today. It would have been quicker to just drive up but from experience she knew that a ride normally meant that Ben had a need to talk.

Ben wanted to get out of the house early to avoid too much talking from his parents. After last night, he wasn't sure what would come next.

Just as they were ready to leave, John appeared, still half asleep.

"Is there any coffee?" He looked around. "Mom and dad not up yet?"

"Nope," Ben replied.

"You'll have to put up with my coffee," he headed towards the coffee machine.

"Did you not go to bed last night?" Emma looked at John while Ben got him a coffee.

"Well, I was going over some ideas and before I knew it, it was past midnight."

Well, that makes two of us, Ben thought to himself.

"We're heading out to get work done. Are we all going to town together or are you going ahead of us?" Ben put the coffee in front of John.

"Thank you. I'll head in early if you don't mind. I'll meet you there. Is that okay?"

"Yep, that's fine. See you later. Come on, Emma, we better get going." Ben headed for the door.

"Hope you'll be fresh for later," Emma looked at John and laughed.

It didn't take them long before they were up on the horses and heading out. Ben hadn't said a thing while they were getting ready but Emma knew that once they were on horseback, he would eventually start to talk. She might have to make a comment to get him started.

"I can't wait to see Maria," Emma looked at Ben to see what his reaction was. When he didn't reply, she carried on. "And you two were so close back in school. What happened?"

Ben was still looking ahead but did react.

"Well, we were never more than just very good friends and I guess she moved away while I stayed." Ben began to wonder why it had never been more than just friendship between him and Maria. They had spent almost every free moment together; their relationship had been more like a sister/brother thing to him.

"I have a good feeling she'll be able to help you."

"How?" Ben finally looked at her. How could she think that Maria could help them save the ranch? She worked in a shop.

"Well, remember, she runs the tourist shop and she knows a lot about social media and websites."

This was all foreign talk for Ben; he had absolutely zero ideas of what that could be useful for. Well, he did know that a couple of the other ranches had websites and he knew that there was something called Facebook but he had no idea how that could help him. It all sounded far too complicated for him.

"Think today is going to be good, Ben, I have a feeling that we'll come up with some great ideas."

"Mom and dad have handed me the ranch."

Now it was Emma's turn to be caught off guard. Talk about dropping a bomb. It took her a few seconds to think about what he had just said. That would be why he was acting odd she thought.

"Really? Why? I mean, great news but why now?"

"Not sure but I think the whole thing about not telling me about the issues and mom being taken ill had made them realize that they couldn't continue like they had."

"Okay, when did all this happen?"

"Last night after you left. They said they were sorry for not telling me earlier about the Bank issues. If I can save it, it'll be mine."

"You will save it, Ben, but you will have to let us help you. What did John say to all this?" She wondered if there had been something happening between them. After all, John wouldn't get anything out of it.

"He seems pretty okay about it all. He said that he had no idea what to do if it was handed to him, but he is very determined to help me. He came down with me last night after mom and dad had gone to bed. He wanted to know what I did during the day, what I'd like to do and what I thought would be possible for the ranch."

"There you are. He is your brother and he loves you and your parents."

"Yeah but why hasn't he been back more then?"

"My guess would be that he has a busy life and as long as

things run smoothly you keep going and forget about time. You know that."

They had reached the cattle. If time could stand still, this was where Ben wanted to be. This was what he loved and it didn't matter if he was on his own– he could never get tired of this. However, having Emma as company wasn't bad either. Somehow it felt good talking to her; she never pushed him for answers. There was sort of an unwritten rule for how far she could go. It had taken him a long time to get to the point where he felt safe enough to trust someone enough to talk about things that troubled him.

The cattle looked very happy eating away while it was still reasonably cool. Later in the day when it was hotter, they would head for the shady parts of the field. Ben and Emma had somehow ended up down by the river but there was no time to sit and enjoy the view today as they had to get back for their coffee meeting in town.

On the way home, Ben could feel his stomach tightening. Why was he nervous about this? After all it was just a coffee meet-up with friends but somehow, he felt that his future rested on what they could come up with.

Back at the house, Bill and Helen were up now.

"Had a late start this morning then." Ben walked across the kitchen floor to give his mother a hug, something he never really had done before she was ill. Now it just seemed like the right thing for him to do.

"Morning, son," she said as she hugged him back. "You just missed John, he left a few moments ago."

"That's okay. He told me he had something he wanted to

do. Emma and I are going in together." Helen and Bill looked at each other and Helen smiled.

"Hello, how are we all today?" Emma came in and went over to Helen to give her a hug. "I'll be back later to help with cooking, so don't you start without me." She gave Helen a smile.

"I won't," Helen promised.

"Have to say you're looking good today, got your color back."

"Thank you. Now, you two better be going. Have fun!" She gave Ben a look as if to say *especially you*. Once they had left, Helen turned to Bill.

"She is such a lovely girl; wouldn't it be nice if Ben could see that too?" Bill looked at her and kind of agreed but also warned Helen not to interfere.

"You know how badly hurt he was when Lisa left."

{ 10 }

Not a lot was said on the way into town. Ben managed to park almost right outside the shop and as he got out of the truck, he looked across to the Bank. There was something fishy about that place and he had a feeling that the Bank hadn't been acting in the best interest of his parents when they took out the mortgage. If only his parents had asked John to help them – maybe they would have had a mortgage with some different terms and conditions.

"You coming?" Emma looked at him.

"Oh yes," he said and locked the truck. "Sorry, was just thinking of my meeting the other day."

As they walked in, Ben spotted John and wondered how long he had been here. He looked like he was enjoying himself.

"Ah, you here, brother," John went over to greet Emma. "Maria has made the room ready for us."

"Hi, Ben. John told me your mom is back home. That's really good news." Maria gave him a big hug. "You still look so gorgeous; bet you have lots of girls chasing you." She then turned to Emma. "Long time no see, my friend," the girls gave each other a hug. "How are you, Emma? You look stunning, I take it Ben is not working you too hard."

"I'm fine, thank you. How are you? Like what you have done with this place." Emma looked round. It had been a couple of years since she had last been in the shop. It had definitely changed a little bit since then.

"Yeah, I'm trying to put my stamp on it so to speak but it's a very slow process. My aunt and uncle aren't exactly keen on modernizing. Now, do you all want coffee?" They all nodded.

"I'll be right back," she disappeared out of the room.

"Good ride this morning," John looked at them both.

"Yeah, not too bad. I think I'll have some calves ready to go to be marked soon that would bring in some cash."

"Good plan, brother. It might soften them a bit across the street."

Maria returned with a tray full of coffee and some cake.

"Help yourself to sugar and milk," she said. "So, I was telling John that I have some ideas I want to run by you all. I've been thinking about how I could help you and it's pretty obvious really when you think about it."

"Okay, how?" Ben couldn't help sounding a bit suspicious.

"Well, I work here and this is a tourist shop. All I need is some brochures and contact details and I can start right away. And as I manage the shop, I won't charge you for advertising – that'll be on me."

"That's very kind of you, Maria. I can take some pictures for the brochure," Emma turned to Ben. "What do you think?"

Before Ben had had a chance to answer, Maria carried on.

"I also spoke to John about creating a website and doing some social media publicity."

Ben looked at them all and had no idea what to say. This was already running out of control as far as he could see.

Emma had spotted his look.

"Oh, that would be good, Maria. Shall we just talk about the brochure first?" Emma hoped by slowing this down a bit, Ben wouldn't go all negative on them.

"Sorry, I'm just so excited about this as I can see a lot of potential in advertising."

"I've told Maria that her help and ideas are much appreciated, and I think she's come up with some perfect answers. Don't you think, Ben?" John looked at his brother.

Ben didn't know where to look, what to say and more to the point, how he was going to pay for all this.

"Guys, this all sounds great but how am I gonna do all this and pay for it all?"

Emma looked at him, realizing that if Ben was going to agree to anything, they needed to take it step by step. So, she came up with a suggestion.

"Great ideas, Maria. Can you just grab me a pen and paper? I'd like to write all the suggestions down and then we could go through them one by one. Think it'll be easier that way."

"Yeah, good plan, Emma. Give me a second," Maria quickly went and came back with pad and pen and handed it to Emma.

"Let's start with the brochure first?" She looked at Ben.

"Yeah, sounds good but how much will it cost and what should I put in it?"

"Ben, first of all, remember you don't have to do it all by

yourself. We're all here to help you, okay? Don't forget that. And secondly, if we go through the suggestions and ideas first and then work out a plan afterwards, some of it might need a bit of looking into. Do you all agree on that?" John looked around. "So, Emma if you would write down all the suggestions for now."

"No problem." Emma put her hand on Ben's leg and whispered to him, "You'll be fine."

The first point was the brochure which Maria had suggested. She explained that with a few photos and a bit of text she could soon put something together that she could hand to the tourists. And to start with it, they could be photocopies printed on normal paper. Then later if it was a success, they could be made into a proper little folded brochure.

"I'll just pop out and get one so you can see what it is I mean," Maria returned with one – one about water rafting and she handed it to Ben.

Well, this doesn't look too complicated, he thought, unfolding it.

"So, what would we put in it?" He looked at Maria.

"Well, the basis would be who you are, what you offer, prices, a small map for your location and a few pretty pictures. If you give me the details, I can do it soon."

"Well, I have a small but very good camera which I could bring out on rides," Emma piped in.

"Excellent, Emma. What do you think, Ben?" John looked at his brother hoping he could see the benefits. Ben who was still looking at the brochure, looked up and across to Maria.

"Will you do this for me or for us?" Ben asked.

She smiled and nodded.

"Then all I can say is thank you so much, and that it's very kind of you. Let's do it." For the first time, Ben actually smiled.

They carried on with social media which was something Ben had no idea about. John had some but it was Maria and Emma who knew how that worked and were familiar with it. After it had been explained and Ben was told he didn't have to do anything and more to the point, it wouldn't cost him anything, he agreed that it wouldn't hurt to try. Emma said that she would create both a Facebook and Instagram page over the next couple of weeks and would take on the responsibility of running them.

Ben was beginning to feel a little optimistic and had started to relax a bit. Maybe, just maybe there was a way out of this.

"Okay, let's move on to the next thing – a website. Now I think this is a must." John looked around at them all. "A website means that people can find out about you without leaving their homes; they can book straight away from their living room or wherever they are."

"Yeah, and we can add in links to other things." Maria went on to explain how they could create links to other tourist activities in the area like the water rafting company.

"Okay, this all sounds like a lot of work and surely would cost a lot to do?" Ben was struggling with this one. "How do you build a website? And who's going to do it?"

"Well, this isn't that difficult Ben. I have a buddy in New

York who owes me a favor and this is what he does for a living."

"Really? That's amazing, John!" Maria got very excited about it as she could see a lot of potential in a website. "If done in the right way so it's easy to manage and navigate, anyone can run it and it can generate a lot of business. I know a couple of shops and small businesses here that have had great success with a website."

"Surely he wouldn't do it for free?" Ben looked at John.

"Honestly, Ben, it won't take him too long to build. Think of it as lots of boxes that have to fit together in a certain way. You have to give him the contents of the boxes but he'll tell you what each box needs. I'll give him a call later and have a chat with him about it."

"Sounds like a good plan." Emma made a note that John was dealing with the website for now.

"Anyone for more coffee?" Maria looked around. Ben looked at his watch. They had already been here for over an hour.

"No, thanks, Maria. I better get back soon – have a small group coming in this afternoon – last minute booking." Ben got up. "But, hey, thanks for the coffee and thank you *so* much for your offer to help. It really means a lot."

He walked around and gave her a big hug.

"No problem. I'll work on some text over the weekend together with John," she looked across to John and smiled.

"And if you could send me some pictures, Emma, then I can put a brochure together, print a few out, and put them on display in the shop."

Emma had got up as well.

"I'll get them done tomorrow and send them to you."

The girls exchanged emails and phone numbers.

"And thanks for coffee, Maria. It was so good to see you."

"You too. Now, take good care of that young man."

"I will." Emma smiled at her and then turned to Ben.

"Ready when you are."

As they were walking out, Ben couldn't help thinking what Maria had meant with that last line. Was he really that bad that he needed looking after or did it mean something else?

"Thanks for doing this, Maria. It's very kind of you to offer your service. Ben has taken it very hard and you know how sensitive he is," John started to collect the cups and plates on the table.

"Leave that, I'll sort it out later. What *did* happen between Ben and Lisa? I've heard different versions."

John told her the story and how Emma had got him back on track.

"Poor guy, but looks like him and Emma are good."

"I know it looks like that but they're just friends. Ben doesn't seem to want to commit himself to anyone."

"Really. You could have fooled me. Have you tried to speak to him about it?"

"Touched on it the other day but not more than that."

"Well, we'll have to sort that out as well." Maria gave John a big smile. "I have to get back to work but do you wanna come around my place later tonight to help with the brochure?"

"Thought you'd never ask. I'd love to. Just give me your address and a time." John was so pleased she had asked.

Maria wrote her address down on a piece of paper.

"Shall we say 6-ish?"

"Should be okay. Will check with Ben and let you know. Shall I bring pizza?

"Sounds like a good plan."

John gave her a kiss on the cheek and thanked her again for the coffee before he headed home.

As predicted, Ben didn't say anything on the way home

and Emma was trying to work out how best to approach the subject without pushing him too far.

"How many in the group this afternoon?" She looked at him to see how he reacted.

"Only four, why?" He sounded a little grumpy but that didn't necessarily mean that he was. Ben often sounded like that when he had a lot on his mind.

"Oh, just wondered if you want me to come along or for me to take it for you."

This time Ben turned his head and looked at her. Wait, was that a smile she saw? But she stopped short of commenting on it.

"Sorry, didn't mean it like that. Why don't you come along just in case they are a talkative bunch? Don't think I can handle too much more of that today."

That's better, Emma thought. *He is loosening up now.*

"Hey, was that a little smile I saw there, Ben Jackson?" She couldn't help but laugh a bit. "You do look so much better when you smile. Of course, I'll come with you or can I take it and you can have peace?"

"Nah, I'd rather be doing something. If I stay behind, I might be forced to talk about this morning and I think that will drive me crazy. And by the way I do smile a lot." *What a cheeky remark,* he thought but he knew she was right in that smiling wasn't something he was known for.

"If you like, I'm happy to go through all the things we talked about with you later."

"Yeah, I'm still struggling to see how it can help in saving the ranch," he shrugged his shoulders.

"Let's just focus on the brochure this weekend. That's very simple and I think once Maria starts handing it out or uses it on the tourists, you'll see what it can do. Trust me. It can only have a positive effect."

They had reached home but before they headed in Ben looked at her and said, "Let's just keep it between us for now. I haven't got energy to explain it all to mom and dad right now, plus we don't have time."

"No problem. Besides, I think it's something you and John should do together, not you and me."

She was right, it wouldn't be right if John wasn't there.

"Speaking of John, do you think there's more than just friendship going on there?" Ben asked.

"Don't know. Didn't really cross my mind to be honest but that wouldn't hurt, would it?" She looked at him and wondered whether he did have feelings for Maria in the end.

"No, it wouldn't," he saw the look on her face. "And just to be straight here: No, I don't have feelings in that way for her. She was and still is a very good friend. Just wondered though. If there was something more than friendship, he actually might be serious about moving back."

"I think your parents would love it if he did."

"Yeah, I know. Hey, let's go and grab a sandwich before the ride." They headed indoors and found Helen and Bill having their lunch. Helen was smiling when she saw Emma was there too.

"Hello, you two. Ben, there will be two more for the ride. A couple called and asked if it would be okay to join this afternoon. They were just passing and saw the old sign up on the road. Think actually we should make a new sign to go up there. You can hardly read the numbers they said. Do you want some lunch?" Helen went to get up but Emma stopped her.

"I'll sort it out, Helen, don't you worry. One or two sandwiches, Ben?" Ben hadn't heard her at first, he was busy thinking of what his mom had just said. She was right, that sign had been up for so long – he couldn't remember ever seeing it as new.

"Hello..." Emma could see he was thinking and wondered what it was.

"One, please." He pulled a chair out and sat down next to Bill.

"We thought that you could either take the two groups together or you could each have a group," said Bill who had finished his lunch.

"Did you enjoy yourselves with Maria?" Helen looked at

Ben and he knew she would be fishing to try and find out what they had talked about but he kept it short.

"Yeah, it was good to reminisce about the old school days but I'll tell you more later. Haven't got a lot of time right now." Emma came across with two plates and they quickly ate their sandwiches before heading out again.

The afternoon went without any drama and the ride ended up being very pleasant with some nice customers who seemed very interested to know about the ranch life.

"That was a good ride. I wish they could all be like that." Ben was busy putting saddles away while Emma was sorting out the paper work, making sure everything was done.

"Yeah, just what was needed. Hey, I was thinking. You know how you were telling them about your childhood and what you do now and how interested they were in hearing all that?"

"Yeah?" He began to wonder where this was going.

"That's the sort of thing we need on the website."

Emma knew there was a slight danger with bringing all this up again but she also knew that it was exactly what was needed. *If only I had recorded it,* she thought. "Tell you what. When we get back, I'd suggest that we try to write down the questions they asked you today. How about that?"

Well, he couldn't really argue with her; after all it was a very good point. The questions had been very good today.

"Okay, but we better do that at my place. Is that okay with you?"

He wasn't sure if she would like that. Emma had actually never been past his front door before. He suddenly had a slight panic – how messy was it? Now, Ben was a fairly tidy person, one of those who put things back when he had used them. This was something both his father and grandfather had taught him from a very young age. If you put things back in their place you could always find them when you needed them.

"I'm not worried about where we do it, I just think it would be very good while we can still remember them," replied Emma.

"I just don't want to have mom and dad involved in it, if you know what I mean," he was pretty sure she could see his point.

By the time they headed back to the house, John had returned home looking very happy.

"How was the ride then? I hear you ended up with extra customers."

"It was good. They were very interested in what we do and asked the right kind of questions but more to the point they listened so I didn't have to repeat everything like I sometimes have to do." Ben went to get a glass of water. "What are you doing now? Where are mom and dad?"

"Oh, they've gone for a short drive. Mom felt she needed to get out of the house for a while. They should be back soon. I'm going in to see Maria this evening, we'll work on the brochure together."

"Oh, are you now?" Ben couldn't help laughing. "Are you sure that's all you're gonna do?"

"Maybe we'll talk about opportunities for me if I came

back but don't say anything to mom and dad," he looked firmly at them both.

"That would be great. I mean, great about the brochure and great if you came back. Ben and I are going to write down the questions they asked today as they were really good and I think they'd be very helpful when it comes to building the website."

"That's a clever idea, Emma. Have you said anything to mom and dad about it this morning?" John had turned to Ben.

"Nope, just that we had a chat about old days. Thought it would be best if we did it together."

"Good plan. Well, I'm out this evening. We're riding tomorrow at what time?"

"Normal time which is 11 and you are still coming," Ben could see John was thinking about whether he could get out of it.

"Okay, what if we talked to them afterward then?"

"That might work well as you and Maria would have worked on the brochure so you might have something to show them, assuming that that is what you'll be doing later. And Ben and I will have done the questions which would be the first step towards the website." Emma looked at them both.

Ben felt his stomach turning a bit. The thoughts of having to tell his parents made him feel slightly uncomfortable but on the other hand, there had been enough covering up around the subject of ranch crises. And if they had to have a chance to survive, they would have to work together. He knew that.

"It'll work for me," said John.

Bill and Helen arrived back a bit later. John informed them that he was going out, came up with something about going to see a film Maria had recommended and that he would grab a bite to eat in town.

"I'll help you with dinner, Helen," said Emma.

"You don't have to. I'll be fine." Helen tried to protest but Emma stood firm.

"No, I will help you. Remember, you have to take it easy," she looked at Ben in hopes of getting a bit of back up. He was busy reading something but did look up as Emma glanced over to him.

"Emma's right, mom." He headed in to sit down next door and left the ladies in the kitchen.

Helen couldn't really argue with both of them. It didn't take that long to get dinner ready. Ben had always been a fast eater and was finished before the others.

"Where did you go this afternoon?" Ben looked at his parents.

"We just went for a drive out to where the cattle are. It was nice to get out of the house for a while. Hopefully, when I see the doctor next week, they'll let me have a bit more freedom." Helen smiled.

But she still looked tired, Ben thought.

"Thanks for dinner. I better start thinking of heading home." Emma got up and collected the plates. Ben had a quick panic – weren't they supposed to work on something? He looked at her and she smiled back.

"Well, I think I'll head down to my place tonight if you don't mind. Could do with an early night."

"We don't mind at all, son. See you tomorrow – both of you."

"Yeah, tomorrow should be interesting. I asked John to come riding with us. Thought he could do with being reminded about his upbringing," Ben smiled.

"Oh, that would be lovely. Well, I'm tired, so I'll head to bed soon." Helen got up and followed Bill to the television.

Once outside, Emma looked at Ben.

"Don't worry, I haven't forgotten about our plan. I just didn't think I'd say anything about it in front of them."

"Oh, I thought for a minute that you forgot."

"They won't notice I'm here if I park behind your house."

"Have you got a plan for everything?" Ben was teasing her.

As Ben opened his front door to let Emma in, he apologized for the mess.

"I doubt that it's messy; I know you too well, Mr. Jackson," she laughed as she stepped inside.

Once inside she looked around. Sparsely decorated with not a lot on the wall. Limited furniture but then again Ben didn't spend that much time here. Apart from a sweater dumped over a chair, there wasn't anything messy about the place.

"Can I offer you a beer?" Ben looked nervously at her. Why was he so nervous? He knew Emma and there was nothing wrong with what they were going to do. This wasn't a date but still he felt it almost was.

"Yes, please."

"That was lucky because that's all I have, I think. Don't really keep anything else here since I eat up at the house every day." Why was he trying to explain all that? Emma knew him.

"Have you ever thought of doing more to this place?"

Emma was walking around. *Not a bad place and wouldn't be that difficult to make it very nice*, Emma thought. "How many rooms are there?"

"What do you mean?" Ben wasn't sure where she was going with this. "Are you thinking of moving in?" The minute that came over his lips, he regretted it. *Man, what are you doing? Don't put words in her mouth.* He could have hit himself.

"No, don't worry. Just wondering," she said laughing. "But do you mind if I look around? I love seeing other people's houses, what they have done to them, and how they have arranged things." She looked at him.

"Feel free or do you want a guided tour? If so, I can do it from here." Ben pointed towards a door. "That is a spare room, the one next to it a bathroom. The door there," he pointed to a third one, "is my bedroom and that has a small bathroom as well."

Emma went and opened the doors to have a look inside. When she got to his bedroom she looked at him.

"Is it okay if I...?" she pointed at the door.

"Yeah but no comments about it." Ben wasn't sure what to feel about all this. That's it. He would have no secrets now;

she would know everything – well, she already knew a lot anyway. *Stop being so silly*, he kept saying to himself.

"And what is behind this then?" Emma had gone to the other side of the kitchen / living room.

"Oh, another spare room and a small one for laundry."

"Very nice," Emma returned. "Okay, let's write these questions down then?"

Finally, Ben thought. He was beginning to think if they were ever getting to that point.

{ 11 }

John was on his way to Maria's place. The radio was turned up, he was singing along and feeling very happy as it brought back memories from the days when he and his brother would head off to parties. They used to have the radio on full blast to hide the sound of their own voices, neither of them were particularly good singers but that didn't stop them. Maria had given him clear instructions on how to get to her house and it didn't take him too long to find it. As he turned the engine off, he glanced at her house. *Not a bad house*, he thought and got out. The door was open before he could knock.

"Come on in. You found it okay then?"

"Yeah, no trouble. Here are the pizzas; hope you like what I got. I completely forgot to ask what kind you prefer." John handed Maria the two boxes and had a quick glance around. It had a very nice modern feel to it and he really liked it.

"You have a very nice house, Maria. How long have you lived here?"

"Just over two years now. And thanks. It has taken me a while to get to this stage. Still got a little bit to do but I'm nearly there now."

She showed him into the kitchen which was a reasonable size with a small table in the corner. Maria went and got a couple of plates, a knife for the pizza and a couple of glasses.

"Don't know about you but I prefer to eat pizza with my fingers."

"Yeah, me too. Can I do anything?" John was stood in the middle and felt he had to do something.

"Yeah, I take it you want a beer; could you grab two of them from the fridge?" she pointed towards the fridge.

"Sure," he went to the fridge. *Wow someone doesn't live on fast food, that was sure*, he thought.

"Well, you won't go hungry any time soon," he laughed.

"I do love cooking; it makes me chill out. Come and sit down," she pointed to the chair.

"Well, good thing you haven't seen my fridge then. Apart from beer, I don't think there's anything else in there."

"So, you never eat at home?" Maria almost looked shocked.

"I sometimes do but it's mainly takeaways or ready meals."

Maria looked at him like 'you do what?'

"I know, not something to be proud of." He smiled. Their eyes met across the table. And for the first time, John could see how beautiful they were. *How have I never seen this before?* He thought.

"How long do you think you will stay here?" Maria looked at him.

"To be determined. I was going to stay for 2 weeks but now that I know about the financial situation I plan to stay and help Ben through it." He went on to explain that he hadn't had a holiday break for a long time and if need be, he could do a lot of his work from here. "The last few days had made me realize that life is more than just work and cocktail parties. Maybe it's time for a change of lifestyle."

"That sounds interesting. Are you serious about this? I mean about the lifestyle change?"

"Yeah, I think so. Please don't say anything to my mom and dad yet as I haven't worked it out myself but yes, I'm thinking of a chance."

Maria reached across the table and took his hand and smiled. "I am liking what I hear." They sat for a little while holding hands; it was as if neither of them would be the first to break free. "Maybe you could come back and work here. This town could do with some fresh input. And of course, it would be good to have you around."

"Do you really mean that? Especially that last part?"

"Yeah, I do. Another beer?" Maria had to let go so she could clear the table and got a couple of beers.

"Yeah, sure. As I said, I'm thinking about it. With mom being sick and the ranch struggling, it might be better if I was here to help. Besides, I had kind of forgotten how nice it is here, how fresh the air is, and I still have a few friends here." He couldn't take his eyes off her.

"Surely you have friends back in New York?"

"Honestly, no, not really, not like us here today. How many years has it been and we just picked up where we left off? In New York, it's all business meetings; even when you meet up socially you talk about business..."

"What do you think Ben will say?"

"I've mentioned it to him and he didn't seem too worried, not that he has anything to worry about. I have no intention of doing ranching if I came back. On the other hand, mom and dad are not getting any younger and having me here might be helpful for him. But you know what he's like. He doesn't like asking for help."

"I think it's more a trust thing for him."

"You're probably right but the fact is that he'll need help to get through this. He deserves to have the ranch."

"Let's go next door? More comfy seats in there," Maria had got up and headed towards the living room. She sat down on the couch. "At least he has Emma," she indicated to John that he should sit down with her.

"Ah yeah, but for how long? Is she going to stick around forever in the hope that one day it'll be more than just a friendship?"

"But it's *so* clear to see, they look so much like a couple. Did Lisa really hurt him that bad? Maybe we need to arrange for them to go and see something – get away from it all."

"That's a good idea. Anything in mind?"

"Yes, I think so. When is Emma's birthday?"

"Well, how should I know that?" John looked at her.

"I'm pretty sure it's coming up soon." She replied and went on to explain what she had in mind.

"Great idea. I'll ask mom about the date." John smiled.

It was rather late by the time John headed home. As he drove past Ben's house, he saw that Emma's car was there and it made him smile.

"Gosh, is that the time?" Emma looked at her watch and it read 10.30. "I better be getting home to get some rest. Thanks for a lovely evening, Ben," she got up and gave him a hug and she was gone before he could say anything.

He had really enjoyed the evening in the end, once Emma had done the tour of his place. He couldn't help but smile. She seemed to like it but also had a few suggestions on what he could improve. Well, maybe one day and that if they could keep the ranch, he would get around to freshening it up a bit.

There was something about Emma that made him comfortable, something that made him feel secure and yet he couldn't see it going any further. She was young and he was pretty sure that one day she would have had enough of this ranch life and head off to do something else. Let's face it, his life was pretty harsh at times, especially in the winter and it was clearly not something that would make you very rich. No, he couldn't expect any ladies wanting to live a life like this. Loving horses wasn't going to be enough.

His thoughts went on to something John had mentioned about maybe moving back here. Was John seriously thinking of coming back? And why? Ben had visited him in New York and seen his lifestyle; moving back here would be a massive change for him. The more he thought of it, the more he realized that part of him would love to see his brother coming back. Well, not on the ranch, of course. Having him around had been good in many ways and with his mother out of action there was more to do. Besides, if all these plans for saving the ranch were going to work, he would need help as he realized that he was never going to be able to do it on his own. He just had to make sure he was in control of it all and that John wasn't just rolling in and taking over. More importantly he wanted the ranch to stay the way he loved it.

As he laid in bed trying to fall asleep, he couldn't stop thinking of all the things that they had talked about. He fully understood the brochure and how that could work for him, especially as it wasn't going to cost him a lot. The website idea he was more skeptical about but mainly because he didn't really understand how the internet worked. It had never really interested him. Did people really go searching for things on there? And how would they find the ranch?

Emma had tried to explain it to him earlier in the evening and she had even suggested that he could come into her house the following evening. Her parents were away this weekend. She would get takeaway and they could have a look at some of the websites and maybe even get some ideas for what they could offer. It was a very good idea and before he knew it, he had said yes. He had never been to her house before. And another evening with her alone. Part of him was really looking forward to it but there was also a part of him that was telling him to be careful; he couldn't face that pain again.

The alarm kept beeping away. Ben put his arm out and turned it off. It felt like he had only just gone to sleep. He had no idea when he had finally dozed off. He remembered seeing the alarm clock showing 01.00. If only he could turn over and stay in bed, but no chance of that today. He eventually got out of bed and started to wonder what the day had in store for him. Suddenly he remembered that John was joining them on the ride today. He couldn't help smiling and thinking back to the old days. Yeah, it was going to be good having John out with them.

Emma turned up as he was eating his breakfast on his own. They were discussing where to go with the group when John appeared still half asleep.

"Late night?" Ben looked at him. Emma got him a coffee as she was preparing one for herself.

"Yes and no. I was back by 10.30 I think but then I decided to have a look at the books trying to work out how much we need to make for it to work," he had a quick look around to see if his parents were there.

"Mom and dad have gone out for an early morning walk so feel free to talk." Ben was keen to hear what he had to say.

"Well, I came across the agreement with the Bank on the mortgage and there's something about it that I'm not sure is right."

"What do you mean?" Ben had to admit that reading that kind of document, let alone trying to see if it was correct, was way out of his league.

"Do you know if mom and dad had any professional help with it when they took out the mortgage?"

"No idea but my guess would be no."

"I'm pretty sure my dad won't mind having a look for you. He already offered to help, if you need any." They both looked at Emma.

"Have you told him about this?" Ben looked shocked. His worst nightmare would be if people got to hear about their problems and his failure.

"Ben, he's a lawyer and I *really* think he could help. He won't tell anyone, I promise."

"That's brilliant news, Emma. Once we get a little more done, we could go and see him, Ben."

Ben realized he might have overreacted a bit.

"Sorry, but I am just very concerned about it getting out there".

"Ben, there's no shame in this, especially if it's due to the bank making a mistake." John looked at his brother.

"Well, I hate to say it guys but we got work to do." Emma got up and started to clear the table.

Could that really be true that the Bank had made a mistake or was that just John trying to sound positive? And yes, Emma was right. Her father wouldn't go around spreading news about them. The only trouble with lawyers was that they were rather expensive so how was he going to pay for her father's service?

Well, he had to put all that to rest for now as they had customers coming shortly and that required all his attention. Between him and Emma they had decided which horses to use and which one John would have. Horses were all ready by the time the two families arrived and even John had made it to the yard. After a short briefing, all the usual about health and safety, they started to get them all on the horses. Emma had remembered the camera and the weather was perfect for picture taking; the sun was shining and there wasn't a cloud in sight. She asked if anybody had anything against her taking a couple of photos on the ride for some publicity which everyone was happy with. And off they went.

They returned a few hours later with everyone happy. It had been a very good trip and the two families thanked Ben for being a very good host. They promised they would be back another time soon.

"Well, that went well and I have to say I really enjoyed it too!" John was watching the two families drive off while Emma and Ben were busy finishing with the tidying up.

"Glad you enjoyed it and thanks for the help," said Ben, not that he had needed him as they had all been capable riders.

"I think I got some good pictures," Emma was looking at her camera.

"You definitely took many." John was laughing. "If you could download them for me then I can take them to Maria."

"You can have them tomorrow."

They got back to the house for a late lunch. Helen had put things out ready for them. She had spotted the ride coming back to the yard and thought they might be hungry.

"So, how was it? Could you remember how to ride?" Helen was looking at John.

"It was actually good and of course I could!" He turned to the food. "This is looking good and I'm hungry."

"Help yourself to lunch. Your dad and I have had ours and I'm going to rest now."

"You okay, mom?" Ben looked at her with concern.

"Yes, I'm fine. Just need a little rest, that's all," she put her hands on Ben's shoulders to reinforce her message.

"Oh, before I forget, I won't be here for dinner." Ben had said it before he had thought about what else to say.

"Oh, what're you doing?" John looked at him with a smile. He hadn't forgotten that Emma's car was still at Ben's place last night when he came back.

"As a matter of fact, I'm going to Emma's to look at some websites to see what's out there and try and come up with some ideas. That's all." He hoped that that had been clear enough. Now he just had to hope Emma would back him up on it.

"Yes, I suggested that I'd go through some of them with Ben so he could get an understanding of what websites can do."

"That's a very good idea," John said and quietly hoped that all this working together could maybe lead to more.

"What is this about websites?" Helen had heard what was said.

"Don't worry, mom; I'll explain it tonight." John got up and went to his mother to reassure her that everything would be fine.

There was no way back now; they had to tell their parents what they were working on. That job had now landed on John as Ben was going out. Ben just hoped that John wasn't going to promise them too much in case they weren't going to be successful in their mission. He himself still had a lot of doubt about it all but he wasn't prepared to go down without a fight. The meeting with the Bank was still very fresh in his mind and the more he thought about it the more he took a dislike to Mr. Miles, the Bank manager.

"You okay if I head home?" Emma brought him back from

his thinking; he had completely forgotten about her for a minute.

"Oh yeah, sure, I can manage the rest of the day. Thanks for the help." He couldn't bring himself to look at her.

"What time do you think you'll be coming?"

Oh, he hadn't thought of that. Now what should he say – better not be too early as that would mean a lot more time at hers. But if he went too late, they wouldn't get a lot done.

"How about 6.30? 7-ish? I'll text you when I leave."

"Okay, that would be good. I will have some time to work on the Facebook page and Instagram. See you later." She popped her head in next door where Bill and Helen were. "See you tomorrow."

"Thanks, Emma."

Once Emma was out the door, they all looked at Ben and he was beginning to feel pushed into a corner in which he wasn't sure how he was going to get out of.

"So, what exactly are you going to look at?" It was Helen that started.

"Some websites." Ben looked at John in the hope that his brother would be kind enough to rescue him. After all, Ben didn't really know what it was they were going to do.

Luckily, John could see that this could backfire so he jumped in and started to tell his parents about the idea of a website for the ranch.

Ben started to head for the door.

"Gotta go and do some things. I'll leave you to explain what we're up to, John." He was in desperate need of some fresh air. As he walked down the few steps, he could feel a slight pain in his left side again. He had felt it when he got up this morning but hadn't thought anything of it. *Must have done something yesterday,* he thought and got on with finishing up so he could get changed.

Before heading into town he popped his head in to check if there were any more bookings.

"Have fun tonight, brother!" John looked at him with a smile.

"Are you taking something to give to Emma?" Helen looked at him like a concerned mother.

"Mom, it's not a date." It came out a bit sharper than Ben had intended but the last thing he needed right now was his mother trying to set him up. He knew how much she loved Emma. He could see that she was hurt by the way he had answered and went across to give her a hug. "Love you, mom, and for your information, I promised to bring beer. Happy with that?" In fact, he had actually put a few in the truck just in case.

"Well, you better be off now as I'm going to cook dinner and need mom's help and advice." John was keen for Ben to get going as he had a feeling it would be good for him. Not only to understand websites and their usefulness but also spending time away from the ranch with Emma.

"Okay, I'm off then. Good luck with dinner and see you tomorrow morning." The door closed behind Ben.

{ 12 }

Not many words were said while John tried to cook dinner but halfway through eating it, Helen put her knife and fork down and looked at John.

"What exactly are Emma and Ben up to?" She looked sharply at John.

"I was going to talk to you about it this evening."

"Okay, you better start then. Don't you think so, Bill?" Helen had turned her head to look at Bill to get some support. John could sense they were concerned and rightly so. All they knew so far was that Ben had managed to get an extension on the repayment of the mortgage.

"Well, yesterday when we met up with Maria, we were talking about how we could boost the ranch income. One of the things would be to create a website. Maria runs the tourist shop and was telling us all about the benefits of having a website. I happen to know a guy in New York who does this for a living and he owes me a big favor. Ben and Emma are going to look at some of the other ranches' websites to see how they have done them and what they offer."

Both Helen and Bill looked confused and John realized that they probably didn't know a lot about websites so he went on to explain how they worked and the opportunities that it could give them in terms of business.

"Ben seems very determined on saving the ranch and I

think we're beginning to make him realize that we're here to help him." John hoped this had helped his parents understand it a bit more.

"What can we do to help?" Helen looked first at Bill then on to John. She had that concerned look in her eyes and John quickly thought that it would be best if he gave them something to do.

"Well, in order to make the website interesting we need to add some history of the ranch so if you could find old photos and write a little bit about the history, that would be a big help."

"Okay, but how is this gonna help us pay the bank?" Bill hadn't really been convinced by the whole thing.

"My plan is that if we can make a business plan for the future, which is something I know a lot about, it might get the bank to reconsider their options. We'll find a way; don't you worry about it. Ben mentioned something about having some cattle ready to sell a bit later which could help as well."

"Yes, the young ones are actually looking very good this year and could end up being ready ahead of time."

"That's good; I can add it to the business plan. Now if you two could work on the history and some photos, we'll sort the rest out."

"But how long can you stay? Don't you have to go back to work?" Helen still had that worried look.

"I can take as much time as I want. I might have to go to back to New York for a few days next week. I got a meeting that I have to attend but I'll be back here before the weekend. A lot of the things I do, I can do from here." John stopped short of telling them what his plans were. He didn't want them to get their hopes up too soon as there were other things right now that demanded his attention.

Ben had got changed. It had taken him a long time to decide what to wear but he had finally made up his mind and was ready to go. Why was this so difficult for him? He knew Emma; they worked together every day and it was a meeting, not a date. Still his stomach was turning. As he was about to start the truck, he remembered that he had promised to let her know when he was leaving. He got an instant reply from her: a thumbs up.

Lots of things were going through Ben's mind as he slowly headed to town and all too quickly, he was at Emma's parents' house despite him never been there before. Emma's directions turned out to be perfect. Now was he too early? Had he got there too quickly? He checked his watch, just gone seven o'clock and took one last look at the house to make sure it was the right one. It had to be as Emma's car was parked outside. He opened the door and stepped out of the truck, had a quick look around as if he was checking no one was following him. Emma had seen him and opened the door.

"Hello. Come on in."

No way back now, he thought but then why would he? She was a lovely girl with a beautiful smile. No, this had to stop. He couldn't and wouldn't allow himself to let his guard down. He remembered the beer before he locked the truck and headed towards the door.

"Hey, brought a couple of beers to wash the pizza down with."

"Well done," she said, showed him in and closed the door behind them. "Hope you're hungry. The pizzas are ready."

"That sounds good, I could do with a bite to eat." *What a stupid thing to say*, he thought.

Whilst they were eating their pizza, Emma told Ben about websites she had looked at. There were some which had given her good ideas, and she had picked out a few of them for him to look at.

"Let's go and sit down next door." They had finished dinner and Ben followed her in. "Come, let's sit on the couch so we can both see the screen," she put her hand out to show him where she wanted him to sit.

Ben did as he was told. *Come on*, he thought, *you sit that close to her back home in the kitchen*. Nothing to worry about, well, apart from the fact that a couch has one large soft seat whereas the kitchen chairs were individual chairs. As he sat there, he couldn't help it, their legs had to touch and he couldn't stop thinking how lovely she smelt, not too much perfume he thought. He hadn't really noticed this before mainly because when they were working together on the ranch they were surrounded by animals. *Right, stay focused, Ben*. He kept telling himself. Emma had got the first website up and a note pad and pen ready.

They spent the evening going through a fair number of websites. Emma took notes on what Ben liked or disliked, they discussed how they could add some of the things that some of the other ranches were doing. The evening went much better than he had anticipated. Seeing what others were offering had made him realize that there were definitely things they could try out but one thing Ben was pretty clear about was that he wanted it to be as close to real ranching as possible. They were so caught up in looking that they had completely lost track of the time. Ben looked at his watch and got up.

"Oh, I better be getting home before people start talking." He laughed but was serious about it. "We have a large group tomorrow morning so we better both be riding."

"Yes, I saw the booking. Don't worry I'll be there."

"Thank you for this evening; it was good to see what others have done. Let's hope we can work something out for the ranch."

"We will and I'll bring the camera tomorrow."

Ben couldn't resist and gave her a quick hug before he was on his way. The evening had made him feel a bit more upbeat about the whole situation.

"Morning. Did you have a good time last night?" Ben hadn't spotted John coming into the kitchen. He was too busy glancing over some magazines and eating breakfast.

"Oh, morning. You're up early." In fact, Ben thought John looked like he hadn't been to bed.

"Yeah, I wanted to try and get this business plan sorted before I have to go back to New York."

"What? So you're leaving after all." Ben could feel his stomach turn and stopped eating. *Here we go again*, he thought. All the promise about helping and then taking off before it is done. He hasn't really changed.

"I know what you're thinking." John looked at Ben. "But before you get too far, I'm only going for a few days; leaving

Monday and aiming to be back Thursday or Friday. I have to attend a meeting that can't be done over the phone. And I have to have a serious talk with Melissa – she won't stop calling me even that I have told her it's over."

Ben felt guilty for jumping to conclusions.

"Good luck with that and sorry for jumping to conclusions. I'll try my best to improve. So, coming back for how long?"

"Well, to be determined. In these last few days, I have rediscovered how lovely it is here. You can see the blue sky and the stars at night – can you remember how we use to stay out late to try and see shooting stars when we were growing up? I feel so fresh and relaxed now, I think the clean air has a lot to do with that, probably something you locals take for granted." Ben could only agree with him and found it interesting that his brother had finally seen the light. "Ben, you are so lucky that you live here. I know you found New York very noisy when you visited me and at the time, I thought that it was just you not used to it. And to a certain extent, that was true but being back here now, I realize how peaceful it is here."

"Really?" Ben looked at him. "I thought you'd find it boring here." They both laughed.

"It'll be interesting to see what I'll feel when I go back to New York tomorrow."

"Hmm." Ben didn't really know what to say.

"I'm seriously thinking of coming back. Mom's illness made me realize I missed you guys. Maria and I had a chat Friday evening about what there is in town in terms of business, finance, investment, et cetera, and it turns out there isn't a lot apart from a couple of small businesses run by elderly men who've been doing it for years and probably not completely on board with the latest. Now please remember that this is strictly between you and me. I don't want mom and dad to get too excited yet. Hope you understand."

"Understood." Ben replied and couldn't help thinking that it sounded like his brother had put a lot of thought into this.

"Maria also gave me something to think about."

Ben looked at him.

"Oh, has she now? In what way?"

"She's something special."

"Yeah, couldn't agree more, she was my classmate in school, remember?" Ben couldn't help but think how funny it was that John had fallen for Maria. Nothing wrong with that; in fact, they were a very good match when he thought about it, not that he was any good at all that relationship stuff.

"How would you feel about having me back here?" John had sat down with his coffee looking straight at Ben now.

This was a question Ben hadn't calculated for. Part of him was still very skeptical toward John but another part of him had also warmed to him. He had to admit it was nice to have him here as long as he wouldn't interfere with the way he was doing things.

"I gotta be honest. In the beginning I wasn't thrilled about it but I'm starting to like having you around and I think mom and dad are too. So, yeah if we can find a way of working it out, it would be nice to see more of you. But honestly it shouldn't be down to me what you decide to do."

"Just to set the record straight. I have no intention of taking over here or running it together with you. I mean, I don't mind helping out here and now but not every day."

There was a sound of movement upstairs, so Ben thought it was best to change the subject.

"How did it go with mom and dad last night? Did you tell them what we are doing?"

"Fine and yes, I have explained to them about the website and shown them a couple. Also asked them to write a piece about the history of the place for the website."

"Okay but do they know you're off again?"

"I have mentioned that I need to go to New York but I also reassured them that I'll be back. I haven't said anything about the other thing. They know I have to go back for a few days but that's all. I wanna be a hundred percent sure before I tell them."

Helen came down the stairs.

"Good morning. How are you both? Emma here yet?"

"No, it's still early, mom." Ben looked at his watch.

"By the way, how did you and Emma get on last night?" Now it was John's turn to ask questions.

"Okay, I think. We looked at quite a few, mainly ones here in Montana and discussed some ideas. I don't want to turn this place into a holiday place where you have lots of entertainment and no dirt, if you know what I mean. For me it's all about the beauty of the nature we have here. But I'll admit there are a few things we could do better or offer. Emma wrote it all down so you can have a copy of it. Oh, and she showed me what she had done on Facebook and Instagram but you will have to ask her to show you as I have no idea how to."

"Fantastic. Glad you're thinking that way in terms of what you can add here and I shall look forward to see what Emma has created. I'll have a catch up with my guy in New York on Wednesday. It won't take him too long to build a website. Did Emma say anything about the photos?"

"She's gonna take some more today."

"I was hoping she would have some for me now as I could take them to Maria and help her finish the brochure so it is ready for the shop tomorrow."

"Send her a message or give her a call. She'll be here soon as I need her for the ride this morning."

"Will do," John finished his coffee and headed back upstairs to get dressed.

Ben shook his head. *Always on the go,* he thought. He never had any breakfast. If there was one meal Ben couldn't live without, it was breakfast.

"Morning, all!" Emma walked into the kitchen with a basket full of eggs.

"Hey, where did you come from? I never saw or heard you coming." Ben had been so busy talking to John that he hadn't noticed Emma's car coming. "John wanted a copy of the photos from yesterday."

"I got them here," she waved a thing in front of his eyes.

"That doesn't look like photos to me." Ben was looking at a small stick and wondered what on earth it was.

As she was walking past him, she put her hands on his shoulders, bent forward and half whispered to him.

"It's called a memory stick, Ben, and I have uploaded the photos from yesterday to it so John can have them. One day I'll teach you about the modern world."

"Good luck with that," John was laughing. He had returned – now dressed and ready to go. Emma handed him the memory stick. "Thank you, Emma. I will head into town to help Maria finish it."

Despite it being a rather large group, the morning ride went without any issues. The weather was perfect and the riders enjoying the scenery. *Couldn't be more perfect*, Ben thought to himself.

After lunch Ben wanted to check the cattle and asked if Emma wanted to come with him. He wasn't really sure why he had asked her; it just seemed like a natural thing to do.

"Have fun, you two!" Helen was smiling at them as they left.

"We're just gonna check the cattle, that's all, mom." Ben looked at her as if to say that there was absolutely no other reason for it.

This wasn't completely true; he had woken up this morning feeling really positive about things after last night but deep down he could feel that John's comment about going back to New York had set something off. Was he really honest about coming back? He hoped that talking it through with Emma would help.

After a quick drive round the cattle, they ended up down by the river and Emma knew that something was up. He had that kind of negative/worried look on his face and she began to wonder what had happened since last night. He had been so upbeat when he left hers. Something was definitely troubling him.

They sat for a while enjoying the view. Not a cloud in the sky.

"I'm going to test the water," she opened the door, jumped out and before Ben could say anything she was down by the water edge taking off her shoes.

"What are you doing?" Ben had got out and caught up with her.

"Don't worry, I'm not stripping off. Only going to put my feet in it." She looked at him with a big smile.

"Be careful; the water is cold and I'm not going in after you," he smiled. Ben had deep respect for the water as it was a fairly fast flowing river and the water was cold, it was coming straight off the mountains.

"You're right, it is still cold but it's fun. You should try it!" Emma sat down to let her feet dry in the sunshine. "So, what is on your mind today?" She had to get him started and put her hand out, tapped the ground as if to tell him to sit down.

Ben reluctantly did and, without realizing it, started to tell her all about his conversation with John and his thoughts about the last few days. Emma listened without interrupting him. It was better he got it all out and then they could talk about it.

"What do you think about it all?" Ben turned his head and looked at her.

"Well, for a start, I think it would be very good if John moved back. He could be a big help for you."

"Yeah, I'm beginning to see that now but can I trust that he would stay? I mean, he's going tomorrow."

"I think I know John well enough to say that he won't just leave you to it now. Of course, he will have to get back to New York; remember, he still has a job there. He'll be back by the end of the week, I promise you."

"I'm so grateful that you don't mind listening to me talking. You're an amazing friend, Emma." He put his arm around her to give her a squeeze.

They sat quietly for a little while with Ben's arm still around her and it made him feel good.

"This is really a beautiful spot here, Ben." She turned her head and looked at him then rested her head on his shoulder.

"Yeah, I've always loved it here." He didn't really know what to do next. Part of him wanted the moment to go on forever but another part was telling that he had already gone too far and he should get out before there was no way back. That little voice in the back of his head kept saying *you know what happened last time*. In the end, the voice won, he took his arm away and went to get up.

"We better get back."

Emma nearly fell to the ground; she had been so relaxed enjoying the moment they had and it left her confused as to what suddenly happened. Here she thought that he might finally have started to let go of the past and follow his feelings. Then the next thing he starts acting like he doesn't care about her. Was she ever going to gain his trust enough for him to let go of the past?

{ 13 }

John came back holding a piece of paper in his hand and looking very pleased with himself.

"How are we all doing?" He looked around. There was only four of them. "Where is Emma?" He looked at Ben who didn't look that happy. A few things went through John's mind but he decided that it could wait.

"She had to go home," that was all Ben said. He didn't really feel like saying anything else and was just hoping that the rest of them would leave it as well.

"That's a shame. I have here the first copy of our or your new brochure and Maria will be putting it on display from tomorrow." John handed it to Ben first who looked at it.

"Well, that looks impressive; let's hope it works," he said as he passed it on to his mom. Helen and Bill were very pleased with it and praised John for all the work.

"We must remember to thank Maria too. How much do we owe her?" Helen looked at John.

"Nothing for now. The plan is to see how it goes and once she has used the twenty-five we have printed, we'll work something out."

The three of them kept chatting through dinner. Ben wasn't in a talking mood. What had happened this afternoon kept going around in his head. It had been so nice sitting with Emma down by the river. When they got back, Emma had gone home without saying goodbye to him. He felt angry with himself that he had let his guard down and allowed himself to get this close to her especially at a time when he needed her support.

Once dinner was over, he thanked his mother and said that he would head down to his place. Helen looked concerned; she could feel he wasn't happy but before she could say anything, John jumped in to save his brother from too many questions.

"I'll walk down with you. Need to just go over next week with you if that's okay." Ben didn't protest it.

Once outside and away from the house he looked at Ben.

"So, what happened while I was gone?"

"What do you mean?" Ben tried to deny that anything had happened.

"Well, you look miserable and Emma's not here so my guess is that something happened between you and Emma today. Am I right?"

"Nothing really happened; sort of," he went on to explain the afternoon, not what they had discussed but the fact that he might had let his guard down and led Emma to believe that he felt something for her. John felt sorry for him and didn't really know what to say. It was clear that his brother had feelings for Emma but also very clear that the break up with Lisa still played on his mind. "Why can't I just let go of the past?"

Good question, John thought, to which he didn't have an answer.

"Do you love her?"

"I don't know. I think so. I hate that she didn't say goodbye before she left, I can't think of a life without her here and I would never let anyone hurt her." They had reached Ben's house. "Feel like a beer?" He looked at John hoping he would say yes.

"Yeah, sure." John didn't like the idea of leaving his brother to himself in this state especially now that Ben had started to open up about his feelings. *It will do him good to talk about it*, John thought, not that he was an expert but he knew from his own experience that when you had a problem it was always good to get it out and talk to someone.

Ben went to the fridge and grabbed a couple of beers, handed one of them to John and sat down.

"Have you told Emma about all this?"

"No, I mean she knows about the past but I haven't said anything about my feelings for her."

"I really think you need to tell her what's going on. Maybe she is the key for you to move on, maybe she can help you. It's pretty clear to everyone that she has feelings for you."

"Really?"

"Yeah, in fact Maria asked me how long you two had been dating. As for mom and dad... Well, you know how they feel about her."

"Maybe you're right, but how do I tell her?"

"Just say it as it is. You can't go on living your life in fear of being hurt. In fact, I think it hurts you more not saying anything. You're a very caring person and you and Emma are really suited for each other."

Ben thought for a bit about what John had said and decided he was probably right; what if it was hurting him more trying to fight it? But how could he be sure Emma would stay with him if he lost the Ranch?

"Well, you might be right but what if we lose everything to the Bank? Do you think she will still be here?"

"Right, for a start, you are not going to lose anything. If we can't get the Bank to agree to some new terms after we have done a business plan and made some changes, I will pay what they want and we will go looking for another bank. Okay? So, no need to worry about that. And secondly Emma will stay with you through thick and thin – I'm pretty sure of it. Otherwise, she would have left a long time ago."

"Do you really think we can do this? I mean, the Bank was pretty clear about what they wanted. I don't think they will accept anything apart from a payment."

"Well, we can only try and if they are not prepared to go with it, we'll find someone else. Ben, you have to think that it will be fine and keep fighting. Where there is a will there is a way."

"I hope you're right." He really hoped that John was right although borrowing money from his brother wasn't something he was keen on. But if it meant that the creepy Bank manager wouldn't get his hands on the ranch, he decided that he would do it – as a last resort and only until they could find another Bank. In regard to Emma staying – well John was probably right there too. Could Emma really be the one that would make him happy for the rest of his life and could he make her happy?

They went on to talk about the week ahead. John was

heading back to New York the following day and he wanted to make sure Ben would be okay.

"When did you say you would be back?" For some reason Ben felt a bit nervous about a week on his own with his parents. What if they started to ask questions, not just about the ranch but also about Emma? He wasn't ready to talk to them about what was going on there even that they might had noticed something. John had been very good at stepping in when things got a bit tricky.

"I'll be back Friday at the latest. Have a client meeting and I got to set things straight with Melissa. Also need to have a chat with my boss."

"Oh, Melissa. Is she still bothering you?" Ben hadn't noticed she was still ringing John and forgotten about her.

"Yeah, talk about the wrong one." John went on to tell Ben how they had met and somehow had become an item by accident. He reassured Ben that after her reaction to him having to go home there was absolutely no future for them.

"Does Maria know?" Ben wanted to be sure that John had been clean with her as he didn't want Maria to get hurt.

"Yes, she does. Don't you worry. This last week I have realized a few things about relationships, what is important and what is not. And that is also why I think you and Emma are perfect for each other."

"Really?"

"Tell you what. Am I right in thinking that it is Emma's birthday soon?"

Ben couldn't remember – it wasn't something he spent a lot of time on if he was honest. "Mom would know. Why?"

"Well, why don't the four of us go out when I come back? We could go and see a rodeo show. Haven't been to one of those in years."

Neither had Ben. In fact, he couldn't remember the last time they went and he had to admit that it could be fun. They used to go to them regularly when they were growing up.

"Shall I get Maria to organize something and we keep it as a surprise for Emma?"

"Deal."

Ben felt a lot better; things had become clearer to him and of course John was right. He needed to have a serious talk with Emma. Just thinking of her made him smile.

John left Monday before lunch but not before he had promised his mother that he would definitely be back before the weekend. Ben and Emma got on with the jobs as if nothing had happened the day before. Ben was trying to work out when and where he could talk to Emma and how to start the conversation. *This isn't as straight forward as John made it out to be*, he thought.

When they came back in for lunch Bill pushed a letter across to Ben. He picked it up and looked at the envelope.

"When did this arrive?" He picked it up and turned it over. It was from the Bank and his heart started racing. As he read it, Emma noticed how his face turned serious and she couldn't help thinking; *here we go again.*

"What does it say?" she looked at him and could see he was shutting down.

Ben handed her the letter and walked out. She quickly

read it. It was just to confirm that they had had the meeting with Ben and that the new deadline for paying the outstanding amount. Nothing new in it as such. Emma handed it back to Bill, she could see that both Bill and Helen were very concerned.

"I'll go and talk to him, okay? It will be fine." She headed out to find Ben. He was sat looking out across the land and hadn't heard her coming. She put a hand on his shoulder and sat down next to him. She could see he had tears in his eyes.

"Ben, that letter only confirmed what you had arranged at the meeting."

"I know but it has just become so real. We won't have the money ready and we'll lose it all." He tried to wipe away the tears that had started to run down his face. "Sorry, I can't help it. I am useless at this."

"No, you are not. You are very good at what you do. It will be fine; I'm pretty sure of that."

"It's not just the ranch and the Bank, Emma. It's also about us, you and me. Don't you see? I know or I think I know how you feel about me and trust me, I feel the same way about you but somehow I can't let go of the past," he had turned his face to look at her.

"Oh, Ben!" She couldn't resist any longer and kissed him, then put her arms around him. "I know you've had some bad experience in the past and now you have all the other stuff going on. I can wait. I won't run away, I promise you."

"I can't expect you to hang around forever for me to sort myself out." He sat up and looked at her.

Emma took his hand.

"If we can get through these next few weeks, we can get through anything. Okay? Now come on, let's go and have some lunch. Your mom and dad are worried about you."

Emma got up and Ben followed her still holding her hand.

"Thank you for being so understanding and patient with me." He wrapped his arms around her and gave her a kiss on top of her head.

"Well, I love you, every little bit of you." They headed in still holding hands until just before entering the house.

Bill and Helen were still sat at the table looking a bit worried.

"Sorry, mom, dad. I might have overreacted a bit on this letter. We'll get this sorted; I promise you."

"Ben, no matter what happens we are very proud of you." Helen had reached out to grab his hand.

"I know, mom."

As he got up after lunch Ben felt the pain again in his left groin, quite a strong pain. He still had no idea what had brought it on and decided to just ignore it. Probably just a pulled muscle that needed a bit of time to heal.

The next couple of days went without any further drama. Ben was feeling very good like a massive weight had been lifted off his shoulders after he told Emma about his feelings. In fact, everything was going well until Wednesday just before lunch.

A car came down the drive and pulled up outside the house.

"Are we expecting visitors today?" Bill looked at Helen.

"Not that I know of." As they watched a man getting out

of the car, they realized it was Mr. Miles, the bank manager. Helen looked at Bill with great concern.

"I better call Ben." She rushed to the phone and dialed Ben's number. In the meantime, Bill went out to greet the manager.

"Hello, what brings you out here today?" Bill stayed calm and reached out to shake Mr. Miles's hand.

Helen had managed to get hold of Ben who said that he would be back straight away, he was only up at the yard. Him and Emma had just come back from checking the cattle.

Mr. Miles was stood on the steps up to the house looking around with a big smile on his face.

"Quite a place you have here, Mr. Jackson."

Ben had reached the house and it was fair to say that he was boiling on the inside. He could see no reason other than Mr. Miles being very nosy for him to come all the way out to the ranch. He had never been that interested before. It could only be to have a nose around to see what he would be getting his hands on.

"Why are you here? I take it you haven't changed your mind." Ben had managed to get past him and was stood in the doorway and he had no intention to let the man inside.

"Well, I thought I would come and see how you were getting on."

"We are getting on just fine, don't you worry. You'll get your money by the deadline. Now if you will excuse us, we have work to do so you better leave now." Ben glared at him and Mr. Miles decided to turn around and get back in his car but not before he had done another little swirl around as if he was scanning the property.

"Looking forward to see you then," he got in his car and drove off at a speed straight past Emma who had to jump to the side so she wouldn't be run over.

"What an idiot! Was he trying to run me down? Who was he anyway?" She looked at Ben.

"Sorry, that was Mr. Miles, the bank manager."

"What did he want?" Emma could see Ben was shaking so she grabbed his hand. "Come, let's go inside," all four of them went into the kitchen.

The mood at lunch was a bit somber. Ben couldn't think of a good reason for Mr. Miles to turn up here, it could only have been to survey what it was he was getting his hands on. He decided that he would have a chat with John about it later.

"I don't understand why he came out here. He has never been here before." Helen was clearly shaken by the event and sat down at the table. Ben could see that both of them were worried. And he was concerned about his mother – this was not what the doctor had in mind when she was sent home to rest. Ben had to pull himself together and stay strong especially as John wasn't here.

"Don't worry, mom. I'll let John know and we'll sort it out."

There was a large group booked in for the afternoon and Ben really needed Emma but on the other hand he was a bit reluctant to leave his parents. He turned his head to look at Emma who was sat right next to him and made up his mind.

"Why doesn't Emma stay here with you this afternoon?"

"Oh no, you need her, it's a big group. We'll be fine, Ben." His mother looked a bit calmer now.

"Are you sure?" He looked at them both.

"Yes, we are. Now you two go and take that group out and we will look after this here. End of discussion."

"Okay then I guess we better get going," he touched Emma's hand under the table.

On the way across to the yard Ben called John just to update him on what had happened.

"He did what?" Ben was a little surprised by the way John reacted but he reassured him that he had informed Mr. Miles that he wasn't welcome. "How are mom and dad taking it?" John sounded very concerned which made Ben feel better in a strange way. It kind of proved to him that John was serious about coming back for good.

"Bit shaken I think is the best way to describe it but they are okay. Oh, by the way Emma and I have started to talk."

"That's very good news. Glad to hear that. Keep me posted and have a good ride."

Emma had heard the last part and looked at him with a big smile.

"So, what have we started to talk about?" She had stepped right in front of him and put her hand on his chest.

"You know what," he said and gave her a little discreet kiss.

They finally got everyone on their horses, checked they were all happy and felt comfortable. Ben and Emma were the last to get on. The pain was there again getting on the horse but he had managed to hide it so no one noticed anything.

"Well, that was another successful one, I think." Emma was smiling as she was sorting out the paperwork after the last customer had gone.

"Yeah, they weren't too bad." Ben went and grabbed the last saddle to put it away.

The next thing Emma heard was the sound of the saddle landing on the floor.

"Hey! Careful with them, they're not cheap."

As she didn't get a response, she headed out to see what was going on. She saw Ben in a heap on the floor and he looked like he was in a lot of pain and was very pale. "Ben! What happened?"

She rushed across to him and before Ben could say anything, she had dialed the emergency. All Ben could say was that he suddenly found himself on the floor in a lot of pain. Once Emma had spoken to the emergency, she called the house. Bill answered to which Emma was very glad. She explained what had happened and that she had called 911 and they were on the way.

"Where does it hurt, Ben?" Emma tried to stay calm and she took hold of his hand.

"Down the left side of my stomach and down into the leg. I'll be okay in a minute. Just help me up." As he tried to sit up, the pain returned.

"No, you stay right where you are." Emma looked firmly at him. Bill and Helen had arrived and Helen looked very upset.

"What happened, Ben?"

Emma explained what she had heard and Ben couldn't really add a lot to it.

It didn't take long for the emergency to arrive and it was now Ben's turn to be put on the stretcher. The paramedics did a quick check over and said that it was probably best if Ben got taken in to have a proper assessment.

"I'll lock up and come in as quick as I can, okay," she bent over and gave Ben a kiss on the forehead.

Bill and Helen followed the ambulance in while Emma quickly finished up and she was soon on her way to the hospital too. Lots of things went through her mind on the way.

Ben got wheeled into the emergency department with Bill and Helen following him in. They were taken into a small room for relatives where Emma soon joined them. After a little while, a doctor came in to see them.

"You'll be glad to know that it isn't too serious. Mr. Jackson has a hernia in his left groin and he will be taken to surgery later to have it fixed. You're welcome to go and see him now."

They followed the doctor in. Helen went straight to Ben, grabbed his hand and gave him a hug.

"You're going to be alright, son. The doctor has told us what it is."

"Thanks, mom. I know." Ben was looking for Emma. "Hey, I'm afraid that you'll have to do all the hard work for a while," he smiled at her.

"That's okay, I do anyway," she smiled back.

After a little while it was decided that Helen and Bill

would head home and Emma would stay until Ben had had the surgery. She promised to call them as soon as he was back in the ward.

{ 14 }

John arrived back in New York Monday early evening. He had arranged with Tracey, his PA to meet her at the office so they could catch up on a few things. He wanted to try and get as much done as possible before heading back to Montana. It had been Tracey's idea about meeting up rather than doing it over the phone or through emails. Melissa had already been in contact as well and he said he would meet her once he had been to the office. He wasn't really looking forward to see her again but knew he had to. Somehow, he had to try and get her to understand that it was over between them. The time in Montana had made him realize what it was he wanted and Melissa was nowhere near that.

"Hi, Tracey. How are you?" She hadn't seen him come in.

"Hi, John. Good to see you back."

Tracey got out of her chair and followed him into his office. She closed the door behind her as there was no need for everyone to hear their chat. In fact, she was the only one apart from John's boss that knew what he was planning to do.

"Mr. Patterson said you could give him a call this evening and I have arranged for the client meeting tomorrow morning at ten with a follow up on Wednesday morning if needed."

"Thank you, Tracey. You've been a star. Don't know what I would have done without you."

"Well, I'm going to miss you here in the office but I'm glad you plan to come back at regular intervals. How was Montana and how's your mom?"

"Great. Do you know what? I thought I had everything here but having been back home I realized that is not the case. I had completely forgotten how beautiful and peaceful it is there and I can't wait to get back."

"Is that the only reason, John?" Tracey had that look in her eyes that said 'I know there is more'.

"Well, I did meet up with an old school friend and had forgotten how nice she was," he smiled.

"Well, she can only be better than that Melissa girl. She keeps calling and asking when you'll be back and I kept telling her that I wasn't sure. She never once asked if I knew how your mother was."

"Yeah, that is something I'll sort out soon. I'm meeting her in an hour at the coffee bar just around the corner. She won't call you again, I promise you."

"Thank you. Do you need anything else from me today?"

"Yeah, have you got the contact details for that web designer guy – Pearson I think his name is? He owes me a favor so I thought he could help me design a website for my brother's ranch."

"Will get it to you in a second." She disappeared out of the door. A minute later, John was dialing his number.

After apologizing for the late call and then explaining the

reason for it, they arranged to meet after lunch on Wednesday.

Time to face the music, thought John as he headed back down to ground level and walked around the corner towards the coffee shop. Melissa was already waiting for him. Just looking at her he began to wonder what he ever saw in her; how blind he had been. She spotted him coming in and waved him across.

"Oh, darling, I really missed you!" She was all over him.

John did his best to try to keep her at a distance and eventually managed to sit down with a table between them. Instead of asking how his mom and family was, she started talking about several things they had been invited to.

"Melissa, stop. I have something to tell you." Before she had a chance to start again, he went on. "I am heading back to Montana on Thursday."

"Again? But why? What about me?" She looked genuinely shocked.

"I am relocating back there to be near my family as they need me." He hoped that would be enough.

"But what if I don't want to move there? You can't just do that." She began to look a bit upset and John couldn't decide if it was real or fake tears.

"Well, I need to be near my family. Listen, we haven't known each other for that long and I'm pretty sure you'll find another guy very soon."

Melissa had now gathered control over herself, got up, grabbed her bags and glared at him.

"Well, you're making a big mistake here." She had made

sure to say it loud enough so everyone could hear her and then marched out.

Thank God that is over, he thought and quickly found some cash for the tip, got up and left. Once outside again, he started to head towards his apartment. He hadn't eaten all day and was beginning to feel a bit hungry so decided that the best thing would be to order a pizza in as he didn't really feel like going out. He sat down with the pizza on his lap and started to search for something to watch on TV.

As he was sat there, he began to wonder how he had lasted so many years in the city. *This isn't a life*, he thought as he was sat there alone but on the other hand where would he go if he went out? His phone went ping. It was a message from Maria. She was just checking in to see that he had got back safely and what he was up to. Messages kept going back and forth for the following hour or so. In the end John had to end it as he suddenly remembered he had to call his boss.

"Got to go. I will call you tomorrow. Love you." He had added the last bit without thinking about it. The reply was "Love you too!" which made him feel so happy.

John turned his attention to his boss whom he was meant to call this evening. Firstly, John apologized for not calling earlier but he had a few things to sort out.

"That is fully understandable, John. How is your mother?"

"She is on the mend, thanks for asking." John then went on to explain his reasons for wanting to head back, including the issues with the bank. Mr. Patterson could fully understand John's reason for wanting to relocate back to Montana but he was reluctant to just letting him go.

"I'll try and think of a way we can make this work. Meet me at the office Thursday morning. And about the ranch issue, email me some details and I will have a look – might have some useful contacts."

"Thank you and much appreciated. Good night." John hung up. He looked around his apartment. There were some decisions to be made now. One was whether he should keep his apartment or not. Well, it kind of depended on what deal Mr. Patterson would come up with. He was too tired to think about that now and headed for bed.

The following day he was straight into an all-day meeting followed by another one the following morning. He didn't have much time to think about things back in Montana until after lunch when he met up with Pearson and they discussed the idea about a website. John had made a folder with lots of notes about the ranch and a few websites that Pearson could look at. He also gave him the memory stick with all the photos.

"This is exciting. Never done a western one before. What's the time frame?" Pearson was looking through all the things John had put in.

"Well, given the situation, as soon as possible. I mean, if you can make the basic frame for it so we can get it up and running then we could always add to it, I suppose. What do you think?"

"Tell you what. I'll head home and make a start. How long are you in New York for?"

"Well, I'm hoping to go back tomorrow night or Friday

morning at the latest." John's phone rang. It was Ben and he sounded angry.

"Ben, what's happened?"

Ben told him about the Bank manager's visit.

"Don't worry, Ben, we will sort it. I have already had a word with my boss and I am seeing him again in the morning. How are mom and dad taking it?"

"Bit shaken but okay. By the way Emma and I are talking."

"Good to hear. Think I'll try and make it home tomorrow night, brother." He hung up. Ben's little comment about him and Emma talking made John smile. *At least something is heading in the right direction,* he thought.

"Sorry, that was my brother. It sounds like I better get back tomorrow."

"That's okay. I'll look at it now and have an idea later today on how long it will take. Shall I give you a call tonight?"

"Deal. Thanks for doing this." John gave Pearson a handshake and they headed off in different directions.

John wanted to get some work done at the office so he could leave in good time tomorrow. Ben's phone call had got him thinking and there was something he wanted to research a bit.

It was early evening and he was still at the office when his phone rang. It was Emma this time. *Why is she ringing me?* He thought as he answered it.

"Hey, how's it going?" his smile soon changed when he heard Emma's voice. It sounded like she was a little upset. He started to wonder what Ben had said to her.

"Sorry to call you, John, but Ben is in the hospital and they are operating on him now."

"He is what? What happened?" John sat up and felt his heart sink. This was definitely not part of the plan.

Emma went on to tell him what had happened and John could hear that she was struggling to hold it together. It sounded like Ben was going to be fine but Emma was clearly shocked by the whole thing.

"Now, Ben is going to be fine, Emma. Lots of people have hernias and get over it, okay? I'll try and be back tomorrow night. Don't worry about the work, I'll help you out How are mom and dad?"

"A little shocked, I think. They've gone home now and I promised them I'd let them know when he's back out from surgery."

"Good. Now would you like me to get Maria to come down to you? I know she'll be more than happy to do that."

"I'll be fine. They told me that he'll be back shortly." Emma hadn't really answered his question so John decided that it was probably best if he spoke to Maria.

"Now let me know how he is and I'll see you tomorrow. Okay?"

"Thanks, John. See you."

Well, that was it; he had to get back tomorrow. Maria answered the call pretty quickly and he explained what had happened. He didn't have to say anything about going to see Emma as Maria immediately said, "I'm heading down there now, John. Call you later."

"Thank you. Ben will be fine but I think Emma could use

a friend." He couldn't help thinking how lovely it was to hear Maria's voice. "And I'll try my best to be back tomorrow evening."

"Looking forward to see you. I missed you."

"Miss you, too," John couldn't stop smiling. He couldn't wait to see her again.

Then he remembered Ben and what had happened. Poor Ben, he is really being tested right now. He would be fine; the biggest problem was that he wouldn't be able to do a lot for a few weeks and that at a time when he really needed the work. *Well, I better pack some work clothes if I have any,* he thought before dialing his parents' number.

Emma felt a bit better having spoken to John. For the first time in a long time, she felt very lonely. She kept looking at the clock on the wall. It didn't seem to move so she checked it with her phone. No, that was the time.

"Emma, are you okay?" Emma had been so fixed on the time that she hadn't noticed Maria come in. She quickly got up and threw herself into Maria's arms. She couldn't hold back the tears any longer.

"John called me and told me what had happened." She still had her arms around Emma.

"I was so scared I was going to lose him."

"Look at me. Ben is going to be fine. He is made of strong stuff, you know that. Come, let's sit down and you can tell me what happened."

Emma told her about the Bank manager, the ride and Ben's collapse.

"Why is this happening to him? It isn't fair. Ben is working so hard and still it feels like everything is against him."

"No, it isn't fair but Ben will get through it because he has you." Their talking got interrupted by a doctor.

"Okay, all done. Ben will be back here shortly once he has woken up from the anesthetic. We'll keep him in overnight and he should be fine to go home later tomorrow. BUT he must rest which means no hard work, especially lifting for at least a couple of weeks. Any questions?"

"Thank you, doctor," Emma felt so relieved that it was all over.

"You are welcome. A nurse will come and get you once he is back."

"There, you see. It's all going to be fine. And don't worry about the work. John will be back tomorrow night, he hopes, and he can help you out."

Emma smiled, "What's going on between you two? You seem to have got very close."

"I don't know, it just happened, I think. I always thought he was a lovely guy but back in high school he had other things on his mind."

A nurse came in to get them.

Ben had been given a room on his own. He was still attached to various monitors and he looked like he was fast asleep when they entered.

"I have some young ladies who would like to see you, Mr. Jackson." Emma went over and grabbed his hand.

"How're you feeling?" She bent over and gave him a kiss.

"A little sore but I'll be fine," he smiled at her and squeezed her hand.

Maria stayed back and let Emma go first. *Well, if nothing else I think this will make them both realize their feelings for each other,* she thought and smiled.

"What are you doing here?" Ben had spotted Maria.

"Well, I had to come and support poor Emma. Do you have any idea how scared she was?" Maria gave him a gentle hug.

"I didn't mean to," he looked back at Emma and gave her hand another squeeze. "Sorry, Emma."

"I'm just glad I was there. What would have happened if I had stayed at the house with your mom and dad?" She gave him another kiss. Then she remembered that she had promised Helen and Bill to let them know when Ben was out of surgery. "I better just let them know that you are fine. Be right back." Ben reluctantly let go of her hand.

"Tell them not to worry, I'll be back home tomorrow."

"I'll keep an eye on him Emma while you're out." Maria then turned to Ben. He knew that look, he remembered it from the school days when she was telling him off.

"Hey, what's that look for? I can't help that I had a hernia."

"No, I know that. But you can start to open your eyes and see that supporting, loving and pretty young woman that is by your side. And don't tell me you don't love her because both you and I know you do."

"I know but I keep thinking back to what happened."

"You can't let that rule the rest of your life. You deserve to be happy. I'm pretty sure that as long as you are open and talk to Emma, she'll help you through it. You two are perfect for each other, Ben."

"You think so?"

"Yes, Ben, I do and I am not the only one who thinks that."

Emma came in looking a bit better. Ben couldn't take his eyes off her and as soon as she got close enough, he reached out for her hand.

"How are mom and dad?"

"They are fine. John has spoken to them as well. There is a ride in the afternoon which I can handle. Your dad will help me get things ready and be there when I come back with them."

"That's good," said Maria, "and John said he would be back tomorrow night, he will help Emma over the next couple of weeks. If you need any other help, let me know and I will see what I can do."

"Thanks, Maria. Well, it's a good thing that we took him on a ride last weekend," Ben smiled with the thoughts of his brother having to do the rides.

"Now you both seem okay so I'll head back home. Shall I let John know or have you spoken to him?" Maria looked at Emma.

"Yes, please, I haven't told him that Ben is out again. Thanks for coming by." Emma went around to give Maria a hug.

"Now no more misbehavior from you, young man," she waved as she left the room.

Emma went and sat down next to Ben's bed again and

took his hand. He looked at her and tears started to build up in his eyes.

"Emma, I am sorry. Sorry for giving you a scare like this but also sorry for being such an idiot."

"Hey, it's alright. You did give me a bit of a scare, I'll admit that, but you are no idiot, Ben." She tried to wipe the tears away from his face but at the same time she could feel her eyes filling up.

"I have been holding back for so long because of the past but can't any longer. I love you." Before he could say any more, she bent down and kissed him and then put her hand on his chest.

"I would walk through fire for you, Ben." She put her head on his chest. He put an arm around her and hoped for this moment to last forever. None of them was prepared to move. In the end, Emma said that she had better head home.

A nurse came in to see how Ben was doing and Emma asked her if it was okay for her to visit Ben before heading out to the ranch in the morning.

"Okay, I'll pop in and see. And fingers crossed I can come and pick you up once I've done the ride in the afternoon."

"Sounds like a plan but you don't have to come in the morning." Deep down he was hoping she would.

"Well, you can't stop me," she gave him another kiss.

"I wouldn't try to," he gave her a big smile.

"Well, I better head home to get some rest now."

As Emma left the hospital feeling a lot better, Ben couldn't stop thinking of her. He missed her already and couldn't wait to see her in the morning. The nurse returned to take the drip out.

"I take it that was your girlfriend, Mr. Jackson. She's a pretty sweet lady, I'd say."

"Yeah, she is indeed." Before he knew it, he started to tell the nurse about his past and their relationship. He apologized for rambling on to her but she just smiled.

"Mr. Jackson, it is better to get it out than bottling it up. And having heard what you've told me, I think you're on the mend now."

{ 15 }

John suddenly felt he had a lot to do as he needed to get back to Montana as soon as possible. With Ben in hospital, their parents and Emma could use his help. The last thing Jackson Ranch needed right now was having to turn customers away. Maria had called to say that Ben was out of surgery, everything had gone as planned and he was expected to go home the following day. It was good to hear that it wasn't any worse than that but Ben would still be out of action for a while.

John did a quick scan of the apartment to work out what he needed to bring with him this time. His phone rang, and just for a second, he was worried who it could be. To his relief it was Pearson. He had made big progress on the website already and was wondering if they could meet up the following day. John filled him in on the latest news from Montana and his updated travel plans.

"But if you can make eight o'clock tomorrow morning at the office, we can look at it."

Pearson was full of understanding and said he would be there.

"Okay. See you in the morning." John hung up and began to pack the things he needed. He wanted to have everything ready to take with him to the office in the morning as he planned to head straight to the airport from work. He had spoken to Tracey as soon as Emma had told him what had happened and she had booked his flights for him.

As promised, Pearson was at the office on time. John was very impressed with what he had done so far with the website.

"Well, you had done most of the work already, John. I only had to make the 'boxes' to put it in. I have built it in a version that should be easy for you or your brother to edit when needed."

"Excellent, Pearson. I have to say, I'm very impressed. Could you email it to me so I can show them back home what it looks like?"

"Thank you. And yes, no problem. I'll finish it before the end of the weekend and email you the details. Hope your brother is okay and that this'll help the ranch."

"So do I. You'll have to come and visit us one day."

"I'd love to. Never been to Montana before. Good luck, and I'll be in touch."

"Thanks again, Pearson and all the best."

Next on the list was his boss. As he headed down the corridor to Mr. Patterson's office, he wondered how he would take the news about Ben's operation. It was beginning to look like a rather lengthy stay for him in Montana.

"Morning, John. How are you today?"

"Well, better than my brother," he replied then went on to tell him about what had happened.

"Oh no, poor fella. Tell him to take it easy. I've been through one of those and it takes time."

After a chat about John's future in the company, he had

made it clear that he was thinking of relocating back to Montana, John went on to ask him for some advice in relation to the issue the ranch had with the Bank. He had come across something when he had looked through his parents' paperwork; it didn't seem right and he knew that Mr. Patterson had previously been a bank manager. John hoped he could give him some advice on where to go next.

"Will make a couple of calls but from what you're telling me, I think you have a case," Mr. Patterson reassured John.

Ben was sat up in bed eating his breakfast. *Not quite the same as what mom cooks at home,* he thought. He looked at his phone: still no messages from Emma. John had sent one asking how he was and to let him know that he would be on the way later today with the aim of being back at the ranch in the evening. He had also mentioned something about the website looking very good. Ben couldn't help but smile at the thought that his brother had to get back into ranch work. *Just as well I did ask him to ride out with us last weekend,* he thought.

There was a knock on the door. Could that be Emma or was it just another nurse coming in? There she was: she had her hair down so you could see the waves in it. Ben hadn't really noticed that before.

"What time do you call this?" He smiled to her and reached out to take her hand.

"Good morning. You look like you're feeling a lot better."

"A lot better now you're here," he pulled her in for a kiss.

"Did you manage to get some sleep last night?"

"Sort of. I can fully understand why mom was so tired

when she came home. It's a little noisy here. Looking forward to coming home. Already seen one doctor who said I should be free to go later today."

"So glad to hear that. I better bring you some clean clothes to wear. Can you wait till later in the afternoon? Got a ride to deal with first. Or shall I get your dad to come and pick you up?"

"I'll wait for you." He couldn't take his eyes off her.

A nurse came in to see how he was, and Emma checked with her that it would be okay if Ben stayed until late afternoon.

"Yeah, no problem. Everything's fine so he should be good to go by then. Maybe bring some loose fitted pants, they'll be more comfortable to wear than jeans. I'll let them know that you'll be in later in the afternoon."

"Thank you. Well, I better get to work. I'll see you later," she gave Ben a kiss before she headed off.

As promised, she returned later in the afternoon with some clean clothes. She had managed to find a pair of pants that she thought would work. As she was heading for Ben's room she ran into the nurse from the night before.

"Come to pick up the handsome young fella?"

"Yeah, hope he's free to go."

"Yes, he is. I'll come and help you get him ready, just getting the paperwork."

Emma headed in to find Ben sat up in a chair with a dressing gown on.

"Hey, look at you. Looking very handsome in that gown."

Ben couldn't help feeling overwhelmed by her happiness; it was very infectious.

"Hope you have come to take me home," he reached out for her hand.

"I have." She handed him the bag with the clothes. "Think I have managed to find you some that would be comfortable; hope it's okay," she started to take it out of the bag.

In a joint effort they managed to get Ben dressed before the nurse came in.

"Oh, you're even better looking now, Mr. Jackson. Here are some pain killers and notes on what and what not to do. If you have any problems, give us a call. The most important thing is not to overdo it, make sure you take it easy the next couple of weeks – and no lifting."

"I better read that as I know what you're like," Emma looked at Ben as she grabbed the papers and smiled.

"Nice to have met you and I wish you all the best. Look after yourself and treat this lovely gal of yours well," the nurse looked at Ben with a firm but friendly look, then she turned to Emma.

"Nice to have met you, too. Any problems give us a call."

"Thank you," Emma wondered what the nurse was hinting at when she looked at Ben.

"Now let me help you get out of here," she went to get a chair that was just outside the door.

Ben was finally in the car and ready to head home. Once Emma got in, she looked at him.

"What was all that about with the nurse? Have you two

been talking about me?" She had her head slightly on the side and her eyes looked so happy.

"Nothing. She just asked me how long I'd known you, that's all." He wasn't going to say that he in fact had had a long conversation with the nurse last night when he couldn't sleep. Ben had ended up telling her everything about Lisa and the break up, how frightened he was of being hurt again and at the same time scared of losing someone again. They had a long chat about it which had felt very good. No, he had to tell Emma -open and honest was what the nurse had said to him.

"Actually, I told her all about us and Lisa and she was a very good listener." He looked at her hoping it wouldn't make her mad. The reply was a kiss.

"Ben, that's the best news I've heard in a long time. Let's get you home."

"Can I ask you to take me to my house, not mom and dad's please?"

"But your mom is expecting you. She made sure your room is ready for you as she doesn't think you should be on your own tonight. And I kind of agree with her."

"I can't be dealing with another night of having someone keep checking up on me. Besides, all those steps... How am I going to get upstairs?" There was no way he was going to stay with his parents tonight, there had to be another solution. "What if I asked John to stay with me?"

"That could work but I have another idea. Why don't I sleep on your couch tonight?"

"Would you do that?" *That was an even better idea,* and one he hadn't thought of.

"Yes, of course. To be honest I thought you'd object to your mother's plan so I packed a bag for me."

What did he just hear her say? Was that really what she said?

"Would you do that for me?" He looked at her but at the same time his inner was in turmoil. He was so relieved and pleased that she would do that for him but there was also a part of him that said *stop, be careful, what are you saying yes to.* He had to try and ignore it. There was no way any of them would let him sleep on his own tonight and quite rightly so. It wasn't as if she was moving in or sleeping in the same room as him. No, it was just a friend helping another friend out if any started to ask questions. Was he ready to let the world know about his feelings for Emma?

"Now I'd suggest you call your mom and tell her what your plans are," Emma had dragged him back to reality.

"Before I do that, I gotta ask you to keep what's happening between us a secret," he looked at her and hoped she would understand why. Emma didn't say anything but just before they reached the drive down to the ranch, she pulled into the side of the road and stopped the car. Ben wasn't sure what to make of it. Would she be angry at him? It felt like minutes before she said anything.

"Of course, Ben. I had no intention of telling the world about this. You seem to forget that I know what you've been through and it'll take time. All I'm asking of you is that when you're feeling under pressure, talk to me. Only together can we get through it, and we will." She leaned over and gave him a kiss.

"Now call your mom and tell her we're nearly home. And just tell her that you're stopping at yours as stairs are an issue for you. She'll understand." Emma started the car again.

She was right. Ben didn't have to argue too much about staying at his and they would bring some food down for him.

Next step was trying to get out of the car. Luckily Emma's car wasn't too low which made it easier but still painful. Ben was pleased that he didn't have to climb a lot of stairs. Once he was stood up it felt good to move a little having spent the last twenty-four hours lying down. Slowly but steady he made it into his house. Emma helped him to the couch where he could half sit half lie down in a more comfortable position. It didn't take long for both Helen and Bill to turn up with a basket of food for him and Emma.

"Here's a bit for you to eat. How are you feeling, son?" Helen was holding his hand.

"I'm fine, mom. Just feeling a bit beaten up – like after a bad fall from a horse. I'll be back in action again soon."

"Don't rush it, we don't want you to end up in hospital again."

"I know. Hey, gotta take this." He picked up his phone that was ringing. Saved by his brother.

"Hey, John. Where are you?"

"Just got off the last flight. Heading to car rental. How're you? Are you home yet?"

"I'm fine and yes, just got back".

"That's good news. Take it you're staying at the house tonight."

"Not really." Then in an attempt not to answer the question with his parents in the room he said, "Oh, so you'll be home soon."

"Take it that you're not on your own." John had a feeling that there was something else, but that Ben didn't want to say right now.

"Yes, they just brought me some dinner. Why don't you come by when you're back? Hopefully I won't be asleep."

"Will do. Tell mom and dad I'll be back soon." John hung up.

"That was John. He's just getting the car so he'll be here soon."

"That's good to hear. Hope he brought work clothes. We had a few bookings for the next couple of days so he'll have to help you, Emma." Helen looked at Ben with a smile.

"Really?" Ben sounded a bit surprised.

"Yes, and they all said the same thing; they had seen a brochure at the tourist shop. It must be Maria's thing they've seen, right?"

"That's good news." Emma looked at Ben as if to say, 'there you are, it is working'. "And not a problem at all with the rides. John and I will manage just fine. We might just need you to check cattle, Bill. And later in the week you can take Ben with you. He's not allowed to drive for a couple of weeks according to these papers here." She had had a quick look through them.

"Well, we better get back up to the house. Are you sure you'll be okay here?" Helen looked at Ben with great concern.

"Yes, mom, and I won't be on my own. Emma will sleep here on the couch. It'll be fine. I'll be fine." Ben was hoping they would leave. He just wanted to be alone with Emma now and he felt very tired. The anesthetic from yesterday was wearing off and the lack of sleep last night had caught up with him.

Finally, Helen and Bill left after Emma and Ben had promised that they would ring them if they had a problem. Now on their own Ben looked at Emma who was sat in a chair next to him making some notes on the paperwork from the hospital.

"Come and sit with me for a while."

"Ben, you look tired. Don't you think you should go to bed?"

In some ways he was a little disappointed in her answer.

"Don't you want to?" He asked, and in a split second he was fearing the worst.

"Ben, I'd love to but you look absolutely exhausted," she got up and went to slide down at the end of the couch so he could rest his head on her lap.

"That's better, and yes, I know I'm tired, but I thought I'd try and stay up until John gets here, if that's okay with you, nurse Emma," he turned his head and looked straight up at her.

"That's fine by me. Just to warn you: I think John will work out what's going on here. No doubt Maria would have spoken to him."

"Yeah, but we just gotta ask him to keep it to himself. By the way, do you really think that Maria's brochure has helped already?"

"I do but hey, no thinking of all that today. Just rest. I'll watch something on TV." It didn't take Ben too long before he had dozed off.

There was a knock on the door which woke Ben up. He went to sit up in a bit of a rush but had to stop because of the pain.

"Hey, don't do that; take it easy, Ben. It's only John coming in." Emma helped him to sit up slowly.

"Sorry if I woke you up, brother." John was stood in front of him now.

"That's okay. Good to have you back here." Suddenly Ben felt all emotional, he didn't really know why or what had brought it on. Emma took his hand and John sat down on the other side of him.

"Hey, brother. It's okay. I'm back now, and I plan to stay for a long time. I'll only be going back to New York for meetings from now on."

"Really? Are you serious?" Ben felt such a big relief hearing that. It meant that he wouldn't be on his own against the Bank. "Thank you, John, you have no idea how much that means to me." He had tears in his eyes.

"Yes, I'm serious about it but for now we'll keep it between us, okay? So, being as you're not sleeping at the house, I take it that you either need me here or is Emma staying?" He looked at them both and knew that he wasn't needed.

"Uh, Emma's sleeping here on the couch as I don't feel like

climbing lots of stairs at the moment." Ben wasn't sure how else to answer it and after all, that was the truth.

"I see," John smiled.

"And yes, something might have happened, but we'd appreciate if you didn't tell anyone about it."

"That's great news and no, I won't. Now I understand from mom and dad that there have been some bookings coming in because of Maria's brochure so it sounds like I'll be needing my riding gear."

"Yes, please I'd appreciate some help starting tomorrow morning. Are you up for it, John?" Emma was still holding Ben's hand.

"Yeah, sure. Well, I'll leave you two alone. Think you better get this fella to bed. Any problems give me a call." John got up and left.

"Right, Ben. Time for you to have some painkillers and go to bed, I think." Ben was too tired to argue with her and with Emma's help he managed to get on to his feet.

"You don't have to sleep here on the couch," Ben looked at her.

"I think it's best at least for tonight," she smiled.

"Okay but can we leave the door open so you can hear me if I have a problem? After all, you are my nurse," he started to giggle but had to stop as it made the ache worse.

"Not a problem." She gave him a kiss and he slowly made his way to his bedroom.

"Nooo!"

Ben woke up with the sound of his own voice. He tried to sit up. His clothes were soaking wet and so was the bed. He could feel his heart was racing. He reached out to turn on the light so he could see what the time was. Two A.M.! Emma came rushing in. She had heard his scream and she found Ben sat on the side of the bed soaked and shaking.

"What happened, Ben? You okay?" she rushed over, sat next to him and put her arm around him. Ben looked like he had seen a ghost.

"I had a nightmare. I could see myself lying on the floor. There was some sort of accident and a big fat man was standing over me saying '*it's over, he's dead*'. Lots of flashing lights and he turned his head so I could see it. It was the Bank manager."

"Yeah, I think that would classify as a nightmare. Come let's get you some dry clothes and I think we'll change the bedsheets too. Where do I find clean sheets?" He pointed at the top drawer. And while she sorted out the bed, Ben managed to get changed into some dry clothes. "Want me to get you a glass of water before getting back into bed?"

"Yes, that'd be nice." Emma went and got a glass. When she returned, Ben had got back into bed. He felt more comfortable lying down. Emma sat down beside him. She wanted to make sure that he was okay before heading back to the couch. Ben drank the water and then put the glass down, he took her hand. "Would you mind staying in here with me?"

She thought about it for a second; it was pretty clear that he was still shaken by the nightmare and to be fair, it was quite a nightmare.

"Let me just go and turn off the lights, and I'll be back."

He turned off his light and put his hand on hers.

"Thank you."

"Not a problem. Now try and get some sleep."

That was easier said than done. The nightmare had brought him right back to reality and all the trouble with the Bank. There had to be a way out of it somehow. The more he thought of it the more he hated the Bank or more to the point, Mr. Miles. There was something about him, maybe it was the way he had looked at him the day he came out to the ranch.

Emma must have felt he was awake and gave his hand a little squeeze.

"What are you thinking of?"

"I'm scared that I'm gonna lose it all."

"Hey," she turned over on to her side and looked at him in the dark. "For a start, I don't think you will, Ben, but if that happens, you can only say you did your best or *we* did our best. Things will work out right somehow, they always do. And don't forget that you're not alone. You have me, you have your brother, Maria and your parents." She leaned over and gave him a kiss, then rested her head on his chest. He had his arm around her; it felt very comfortable. She was of course right; he had to believe that they could do it.

{ 16 }

As the alarm went off, he found himself cuddled into her. It felt so nice that he didn't really want to end it but the alarm wouldn't stop.

"Morning," Emma turned her head and looked at him. "Any more nightmares?"

"No, only sweet dreams."

As they laid there looking at each other, Ben couldn't help thinking how stupid he had been, trying to stop this from happening. Why had he spent the last year or so trying to deny his true feelings? He promised himself that from now on, that had to stop.

"Tell me what you're thinking," Emma put her finger on his nose.

"Well, you have the most beautiful smile and you need to get up and go to work," he smiled and gave her a kiss.

"What are you gonna do all day? Lie down here all alone?"

"Well, I was told to take it easy but no, I was thinking of trying to get up to the house. Think I might go crazy if I stay here all alone. You know what my brain is like."

"Good plan. Besides, I think your mother would like to spoil you a bit," she smiled and got out of bed. "Do you want some painkillers now before you start moving around? I personally think it'd be a good idea."

"Yes, please." Ben had managed to sit up. He was still feeling sore but it wasn't as bad today. He got up, stood for a little while and then made his way to the bathroom.

Half an hour later and they were on the way up to the house. Emma had suggested that instead of him using all his energy on walking, she would drive him up today. Before getting back out of the car Ben turned to Emma and said:

"Can we not say anything about the nightmare? I don't need them all to know about it."

"Fully understand you; I won't say a word."

They walked into a kitchen smelling of fresh coffee.

"Morning, you two. How're you feeling today, Ben? Did you sleep okay?"

"I'm fine, just a little sore and yeah, slept alright. Kept waking up when I wanted to turn over because it was painful." Well, Ben hoped that would cover him if he was feeling tired later and it was partly true.

"I suggested that he got up and stayed up here while I'm out. So, where's my ranch hand then? Still in bed?" There was no sign of John yet but there was movement upstairs.

"I heard that. On my way." Soon after, John appeared in the doorway. "Morning, all."

Having finished breakfast John wanted a quick chat with Ben about the website. Pearson had just sent it through on an email and John thought it would be a good distraction for Ben. He could use the morning to look through it so they could discuss it later. Ben slowly made his way in next door so he could sit down a bit more comfortably. In the meantime, John went and got his laptop and got it ready for Ben.

He quickly explained what Ben had to do and how to work it before Emma dragged him away.

"Have fun out there!" Ben couldn't help feeling a bit jealous as he watched John trot off with Emma. Hopefully it wouldn't be too long before he could get back out there.

"Another coffee?" Helen had found a blanket to put over him.

"No, thanks mom but a glass of water would be good." *Now, how do I do this then?* Ben thought, looking at the front page of the website. It was a nice picture of him and Emma on their favorite horses up on the hill looking out over the land. John must have taken that picture the other day when he came out with them but never mentioned anything about it.

Ben's morning went with looking at the website in between dozing off to sleep. He was to his surprise still very tired even though the nurse had told him that he could expect that for the next couple of days. Looking at a computer screen didn't really help either. Every time he had dozed off the phone rang and woke him up.

"Who are all these calls, mom?" She was yet again coming back from the office having taken another booking.

"Well, people seem to have discovered us again. There's now a ride every day next week. It seems like we're back to normal now," she sat down to rest for a little.

"That's amazing. Do you really think that it is because of the brochure?"

"I do and I wish we had thought of that sooner." Ben could see she was feeling guilty.

"Well, we can't change the past so no good thinking of that." As he said it, he couldn't help thinking that he himself was guilty of doing exactly that. "But I feel bad about you having to do all the running. You're meant to rest too, remember? Why don't you bring the phone in here and the diary so I can answer it?" Ben was getting a bit concerned that his mother was doing too much and not taking time out.

"Oh, never thought of that. I'll go and get it now."

Bill came back in after having helped the other two off on the ride and checked the cattle.

"How are things out there, dad? Did they get off okay? And are the cattle okay?"

"Yeah, all fine, Ben. No need to worry. Emma and John have it all under control."

Ben could feel he was beginning to feel a bit restless and was just about to try and stand up when his phone rang. It was Maria.

"Hey, are you checking up on me?" He couldn't help laughing even though it hurt a bit.

"Yeah, just thought I'd hear how you were doing. Is it going okay?"

"I'm okay, just a bit frustrated that I can't do anything."

"How about I stop by this afternoon for a while? John tells me they're having another ride today."

"That's very kind of you but you don't have to," he replied even though deep down he thought it would be lovely to speak to someone else other than his parents.

"I have the afternoon off so I'll see you later," she said and hung up.

"What was all that about?" Helen looked at him.

"Oh, it was Maria. She says she's coming out to see me. Apparently, she has the afternoon off." Before Helen could say anything else, Emma and John returned, ready for some lunch.

"How's it going? You okay?" Emma was stood behind Ben with her hand on his shoulder. She squeezed it a bit discreetly so no one noticed. He looked up at her and smiled.

"I'm fine. Maria tells me she is coming out to see me after lunch."

"That would be good. Shall I help you up?" She went around and gave him a helping hand. As he stood up, he had to restrain himself from putting his arms around her even though she was right in front of him. Instead, he started to head slowly towards the kitchen with Emma's support which he didn't really need but no one knew that.

Lunch went far too quickly and soon Emma and John had to get back out but before they did John wanted to know what Ben's thought was on the website. All Ben could say was that it looked good but he was no expert on the matter.

As promised, Maria turned up shortly after two o'clock. Helen was so pleased to see her and invited her in for a coffee.

"Okay, make it a quick one. I was thinking the patient could do with some fresh air so was going to take him out for a bit if that's okay with you."

"That would be nice for you, Ben." Helen gave Maria her coffee. They were still sat at the kitchen table. Ben couldn't wait to get outside. Maria soon finished her coffee and turned to Ben.

"Where do you wanna go?"

He had an idea but the question was if he could manage to walk that far.

Slowly they reached his log and sat down.

"Oh my god, Ben, what a view from here! I don't remember ever sitting here when we were younger." Maria turned to him. "I can see why you like this spot."

"Yeah, I know. Quite a view, isn't it? To tell you the truth I have only come to appreciate it the last few years. This is one of my places to go to when I need to think." Ben kept looking ahead, he felt a little overwhelmed and thought for a bit about what to say. Should he or shouldn't he tell Maria? So much had gone on that he felt the need to talk to someone other than Emma about it. She probably already knew as she had seen them at the hospital.

"I need to tell you something." Ben had turned his head and was looking at her.

"I think I know," she smiled and took his hand. "Have you and Emma finally talked?"

"Yeah, sort of," he went on to tell her what had happened the last twenty-four hours and how good he felt about it. He also mentioned the nightmare and made her promise that she wouldn't say anything to anyone.

"Ben, you've been through a lot and no one says the next few weeks will be easy but you can do this, especially with Emma's support. And don't forget, John and I are here for you too."

"There you are," it was Emma coming around the corner. The sight of Ben and Maria sitting close made her feel both happy but also a bit worried – well, worried wasn't the right kind of word, she knew that the pair of them had been close years ago and perhaps there was a tiny bit of her that feared that their friendship, now restarted, could become more than just friendship. On the other hand, it was good to see that he was talking to others than just her, she thought. She walked across to them and sat on the other side of Ben. "How's my patient doing?" Ben smiled and took her hand.

"I'm doing just fine thanks to Maria. She was the one that suggested I needed some fresh air."

"Think he is on the mend," Maria looked at Emma and smiled. "But maybe we should try and get you back in again, we have been out here for a while now."

John appeared around the corner. "So, this is where you're all hiding."

As they slowly made their way back, Maria suggested that they all come to her house for dinner the following evening.

"You'd be up for that, Ben?" They all looked at him.

"Yeah, as long as you have a comfy chair," he tried to laugh but could feel the pain. Emma looked concerned.

"Shall I get the car?"

"No, I'll be fine as long as I don't laugh."

Finally back in, Maria said goodbye to Helen and Bill and left. John followed her out to her car. Ben felt very tired after the fresh air and Emma suggested that he had a little rest while she was helping Helen with dinner. Somehow, he had got through the day and was looking forward to get back to his place where he could be alone with Emma.

"See you tomorrow morning."

"Okay. No need to rush in the morning. Only one big group in the afternoon."

"In that case why don't I bring you breakfast and we can look at a few things together?" John wanted to talk to Ben about the information his boss had given him but Ben looked so tired that he decided it could wait until the morning. The other thing was that he felt it would be best if his parents didn't hear it to start with as it would only make them more concerned.

"Okay but don't be too late. I don't do hungry very well." And on that note Ben slowly made it out of the house and into Emma's car. He was so glad he didn't have to walk.

They had hardly got inside and closed the door before Ben put his arms around Emma.

"I've been wanting to do this all day," he admitted, and they kissed.

They were stood like that for what seemed like forever until Emma said, "Come let's see what's on TV tonight." She took Ben's hand and led him to his couch.

"Do you want anything?"

"Yeah, a glass of water and a couple of painkillers, I guess," he sat down. Emma returned with the water and tablets.

"Was it good to chat with Maria?" Emma had sat down so Ben could rest against her with his feet up. She somehow felt she needed to know what they talked about even though she kept saying to herself that she had nothing to worry about. Ben was feeling a bit sore where they had done the operation but it was definitely getting better. He looked up at Emma and couldn't help feeling so lucky that he had her.

"Yeah, it was good," he paused for a bit and then decided to tell her all of what they had spoken about. His past, the nightmare, his feelings for her and also the ranch.

"Gosh, you covered a lot," and as she was stroking his head brushing his hair back, she couldn't help thinking how silly she had been. Maria was just a good friend and that was all. It felt so good to hear it and part of her was very proud of him for actually opening up to someone else than just her. They sat like that for what seemed like hours and Ben wanted it to never end but, in the end, Emma suggested that he ought to go to bed. She definitely needed some sleep as she had work to do the following day. Reluctantly, he let her get up.

"Now let's get you into bed," she put her hand out to help him get up. As he stood there right in front of her, he looked her straight in the eyes.

"Stay with me tonight, please."

Emma looked at him, kissed him and then whispered. "You sure?"

"Yes. I don't want to spend another night without you by my side."

"Come on then. Let's go to bed" She took his hand.

Ben had had a very good night's sleep with no more nightmares. When the alarm went off, he found himself wrapped around Emma and it felt so good. What a way to start the day, a kiss from the most amazing girl. Yeah, he was a lucky man. They eventually got up. Ben had managed to find some mugs but realized that he didn't have any coffee.

"I'll go up and get it," Emma was ready to head out of the door.

"No, let's just send my brother a message to bring coffee. That way he'll also know that we are waiting," Ben couldn't help smiling. "Hey, if you have to stay here and look after me, I think we need to do some shopping, don't you think so?"

This was the first time in all the years that he had lived in the house that he had thought of shopping. He was trying to think how long it had been. It had originally belonged to his grandparents. When granny had died six years ago, it had seemed natural for Ben to take it on. He looked around and thought it could really do with a facelift. Maybe he could make a start now while he couldn't take part in any of the outdoor work.

"Might be a good idea, maybe if John doesn't stay too long, we could check things out at the local grocery store this morning."

Ben looked at her a little confused about what she meant but then remembered.

"Yeah, we could."

"Hey, what else were you thinking of?" She had noticed his confusion.

Ben took a deep breath; should he, or shouldn't he? Then he decided to let her in on his thinking about giving the house a small make-over.

"That could and would be good as long as you don't overdo it. Maybe your dad can help you a bit."

There was a knock on the door. *Finally, breakfast has arrived*, Ben thought and Emma went to open the door.

"Morning to you two..." John stopped short of saying love birds as he wasn't completely sure how Ben would take that. "How are we all today?"

"Fine but starving. What took you so long?" Ben looked at his brother with a big smile.

They chatted away over breakfast and afterwards John wanted to do a quick run through of the website. Emma hadn't seen it yet. John asked Ben what he thought of it and took notes. Once that was done, he had one more thing he wanted to talk about.

"I had a word with my boss regarding the Bank and the mortgage certificate. He used to be a bank manager so I thought I would use his expertise. Now he's come back to me and said that we should seek some professional help as there are some errors in it, he thinks."

Ben could immediately feel his anger brewing.

"Okay but how are we going to pay for that? They're expensive."

"Well, not all of them. My dad will help you." Emma looked at them both. "I'm pretty sure that he will be more than happy to help you out at a special price."

"Are you sure?" Ben looked at her thinking how much she had told her father about the issue.

"That would be perfect. We'll have to call him Monday

morning and book a time. Could you give me his number, Emma?" John was ready with his phone.

"Wait, if anybody is going to call him, it'll have to be me." Ben looked at Emma, searching for some sort of support from her.

"You know what," said Emma. "We'll have to go by my place tonight when we're going to Maria for dinner. Maybe you could mention it to him then. That might put your mind at rest, Ben."

"That would be a good idea." John had got up. "Well, I better head back up, I need to do a few things before work this afternoon."

"Okay. I'll bring this up later. Now could you let your parents know that we'll just head into town for a little shopping? We'll be back before lunch," said Emma.

"Okay, will do." John looked at them both but decided not to make any comments on it for now.

Ben couldn't remember when he last had been in a grocery store but luckily Emma knew her way around so they got it done fairly easy and without too much walking.

Back home again they sat down with a coffee – the first one that Ben had made in his house since moving in.

"So, what should I do first?" Ben looked at Emma who for a minute wasn't sure what he was talking about.

"Oh, yeah, why don't you start with a spare room and see how it goes?"

That seemed pretty logical to Ben. The next question was to decide what to do in there and how far they should go. After all there was a limit to how much Ben could and should be doing but a little spruce up wouldn't hurt. Ben's phone rang. It was his mother who was wondering if they were coming up for lunch.

"Oh, forgot about the time. Sorry, mom. We'll be on our way now."

"Do you want to walk or shall I drive?" Emma looked at him.

"I'll walk. I don't have to rush back." Time for one last kiss before they headed up to the house. Ben resisted the temptation to hold on to Emma even though that he had a good reason on medical grounds but the thought of his mother watching them and the questions that she would ask stopped him from doing it.

"So, what have you two been up to? John said something about shopping?"

"Yeah, I thought it would be about time that I had other things than beers in the fridge, mom," he was hoping she wasn't going to question him too much over it.

"I think that's excellent news but you will still come here for meals, right?"

"Yeah, I'm not taking up cooking, mom," he laughed and at the same time felt relieved that she had taken it that way.

John and Emma disappeared after lunch and Ben went to sit down for a while. He fell asleep; all the walking had taken its toll on him which he found strange as he considered himself to be very fit. The doctors had mentioned that because of the anesthetic, he would find himself getting very tired the first couple of weeks. This was perfectly normal; they had told him. He woke up when the phone rang about an hour later.

His mother came in with a coffee for his father and asked if he would like one too to which he said yes.

"So, how's it going with you and Emma?"

Ben nearly dropped his coffee and for a minute he didn't really know what to say.

"What do you mean?" At the same time, he was trying to think if she could have seen or heard anything, maybe John had said something despite him telling him not to.

"Well, you seem to be spending a lot of time together and you look happy too."

"Well, she's just helping me out. I shouldn't really be on my own, the doctors said, so she offered to stay. That's all."

He hoped that would be enough to satisfy his mother. Helen on the other hand thought or knew that there was more going on but decided that now wasn't the time to push for more questions. She was just pleased that they spent time together – it was almost like fate has pushed them together.

Ben was so pleased when John and Emma returned as it meant he could escape from any more interrogation from his mother. They discussed how they should get to Maria's for dinner; to drive in one or two cars and ended up opting for two as Ben wasn't sure how long he could last. Besides, there was the fact that Emma had to go via her parents to get changed.

"Have a lovely evening, you two!" Helen smiled as she watched them walk down towards Ben's house.

"What're you smiling at, mom?" John had noticed how happy she looks.

"Oh, it's nothing I just think it's so nice that Ben and Emma are spending so much time together. They seem so happy."

John couldn't agree more but he did warn his mother not to push it.

"Give it time and it'll work out. Remember, Ben is still in doubt about the ranch and its future even though I keep saying it'll be fine. And it will be, I promise you. We just have to get through the process." He thought for a second about whether to tell them what his boss had said. It would be risky but on the other hand he had to let them know how they were getting on. "My boss, who's a former Bank manager told me that we should get some legal advice, so Ben is going to contact Emma's dad on Monday. And before you say anything, Emma is pretty sure he will be doing it at a favor rate as it's us."

"Does he think that there's something wrong with it?" Bill was looking concerned.

"He hasn't seen the paperwork, only heard it from me. He did ask if you had any legal advice when you took out the mortgage."

"No, we were told that wouldn't be needed; in fact, Mr. Miles said that would just be a waste of money."

Well, this is interesting, John thought and this last bit of information only added fuel to his speculations.

"Well, hopefully Mr. Anderson can see us next week and we can get this sorted. Now don't you worry about it. Okay?"

He looked at his watch. "Hey, I better get changed and head to Maria's. She may not be too happy if I'm late tonight," he gave his mom a kiss on the cheek and headed up the stairs to get changed.

"I have a feeling he likes Maria," Helen looked at Bill and smiled.

"Yeah, it does seem that way." Bill carried on reading his paper.

{ 17 }

"Just got to pack my bag then I'm ready."

"What? Are you not staying tonight?" Ben was stood ready at the door looking a bit confused. What did she mean by packing her bag? Emma returned and could see the worry in Ben's eyes.

"Don't worry, I need to get some clean clothes. Remember I haven't got my whole wardrobe here," she gave him a kiss and grabbed her keys. "Right, let's go and see my parents."

It suddenly dawned on Ben that he was actually going to see her parents; it would be the first time in years, but not as a school friend. This time was slightly different as far as he was concerned. He was sort of dating their daughter but they didn't know or hadn't been told; did they have any idea what was going on? This wasn't going to be easy he felt and on top of that he had to ask Mr. Anderson if he would be kind enough to help them.

Ben's worries hadn't gone unnoticed with Emma. She could see he was a bit tense; his cheeks were hollow like he was trying to eat them and she knew he would be worried about meeting her dad.

"Relax, Ben, dad will be more than happy to help you out."

"I'm sure but what about us? Is he going to start asking questions? I can't lie to him."

"He won't ask questions about that; it'll be more about how you're getting on as he had a similar thing happen to him years ago," she stopped short of saying that her mother might say something but if that happened, she would deal with it. *There was no need to feed that worried brain any more* she thought as she glanced across to Ben and smiled.

"Right, we're here. Come on. I need to get changed," she got out of the car. Ben was a bit slower; he was getting better at moving in and out her car, it was less painful now as long as he didn't rush things.

Emma opened the door and walked in.

"Hello! We're here!"

Mr. and Mrs. Anderson came to greet them.

"Hello and welcome, Ben. You haven't changed a bit since we last saw you. Still a handsome young fella. Come on in." Mrs. Anderson showed him the way.

"Good evening, Ben, how are you getting on after the operation?"

"Fine, getting there. Hopefully I'll be back in action soon."

"Now don't rush it, my friend. I speak from experience. So, how are things on the ranch?"

Ben was slightly thrown by the question; *nothing like getting straight to the point,* he thought. Had Emma said anything?

"Uh fine. My brother's back helping out while I'm out of action."

"Have a seat, Ben. How's your mother?" Mrs. Anderson had shown him to a chair and Ben sat down as he felt that was the polite thing to do even though they didn't plan to stay long. He wasn't quite prepared for all the questions and prayed that Emma wouldn't be too long, so she could back him up or even better, move things on.

"She seems fine now. The medication seems to have done the trick."

Emma returned looking stunning. Ben couldn't remember the last time he had seen her in other clothes than work clothes.

"So, how's it going here?" She looked at Ben as to see if he had asked her father about the help. Ben took a deep breath. *Come on, how hard can it be,* he thought.

"Actually, Mr. Anderson, I have a question for you."

"Okay let me hear it."

Ben looked up at Emma and thought for a second how he was going to do it.

"Well, you asked about how things were going on the ranch. The thing is we have a minor issue with the Bank and my brother seems to think that we should get some professional help," he had stopped short of saying that they were about to be kicked off the ranch hoping that what he had said would be enough.

"Would this have anything to do with a certain Mr. Miles?" Mr. Anderson suddenly looked serious, and Ben was fearing the worst.

"Uh, yes, it is," he looked at the floor and wished he could somehow vanish from the room. This was so embarrassing, he thought – *why did I agree to do this?*

"Son, I'll be more than happy to help you. Give my office a call Monday morning and book a time. And if you could bring me all the paperwork before our meeting, I can have a look at it." Emma who was stood behind Ben's chair put her hand on his shoulder as to say 'there you go, I told you so'.

"Thank you; that is very kind of you."

"And son, don't worry about payment. We'll sort something out. Now don't you two have somewhere to be?"

"Yes, we do and we better get going. Come on, Ben." Emma turned to her mother who had got up.

"I'll call in one day during the week."

"Okay. Don't worry about us, we're fine. Make sure that patient of yours doesn't overdo it," she gave Emma a hug and then turned to Ben who had got up. "Really nice to see you again, Ben. Look after yourself and hopefully we'll see you soon."

"Thank you, Mrs. Anderson. I will." Ben put his hand out but Mrs. Anderson gave him a hug instead.

"Good to see you, Ben, and we'll speak next week. And don't you worry about it," said Mr. Anderson as they shook hands.

"Well, there you are, that wasn't so bad." Emma looked at Ben as he slowly got back in the car. "You can relax now." She took his hand and gave it a little squeeze.

Maria's place wasn't that far from Emma's and now that they had left her home he was actually beginning to look forward to the evening.

John and Maria had done most of the cooking by the time Emma and Ben arrived, just the barbeque left to do which John was in charge off.

"What did Mr. Anderson say? Did you ask him?" John had been wondering whether Ben would get round to ask.

"Yeah, and he's fine, more than happy to help us. I have to call his office Monday morning and arrange it."

"That's great news. What would you two like to drink?"

"Something soft for me as I'm driving."

Ben looked at her and felt a bit sorry for her but he also knew that she wasn't that keen on alcohol.

"I'll have a beer, I think one is allowed now," he looked to see if nurse Emma would object to it.

"Come, let's go outside. Johns in charge of cooking the meat and the rest of us can sit down and watch him work," Maria headed out into her small garden and Emma followed with Ben right behind her. He was beginning to feel very relaxed and for once he didn't really mind if John and Maria saw his feelings for Emma. *Maria knew anyway so why not just enjoy it*; he went to sit down next to Emma holding her hand. She turned her head and looked at him with a smile. *This feels good*, he thought.

The talk almost immediately went on the ranch and the rescue plan with the website, the brochures and Emma's dad.

In the end, Maria said, "Stop. I think we've done all we can for now and it has shown a little improvement so let's leave it at that and let's have some fun this evening."

"Well said, Maria. So, John, how far are you with your plans about moving?" Emma gave Maria a look and a big smile.

"Well, as a matter of fact I'll be coming back to Montana,

but I won't move back to the ranch." The way he and Maria looked at each other said it all.

"John and I have connected and why waste more time? It seems pointless for John renting or buying something and not using it so he will be moving in here." Ben nearly dropped his beer. *Well, talk about moving at speed*, he thought.

"Moving in here, you say? Do mom and dad know this?"

"No, I haven't said anything as I haven't really had time but my plan is to tell them this coming week." John was looking very happy sat there with an arm around Maria's shoulder. It was pretty clear that this was more than just friendship. Ben wasn't sure what to feel. She had been his best mate through most of his school life but that was all.

"So, what about New York and your job then? I thought you loved that place?" Ben had never heard John say anything negative about the big city.

"I thought I did but then mom's illness made me realize that there's more to life than wine bars, cocktail parties, and all that. And it turns out this place could do with some new input in investments. I've had a word with my boss and he is happy for me to work from here as long as I come to New York every so often."

"That's amazing and you can always help out when my co-rider falls ill." Emma gave Ben a gentle push. "Sorry, I couldn't help it." He looked at her and put his arm around her to give her a squeeze.

"So just to be clear, is Emma the nurse or is there more going on here?" John winked at Ben who felt the color of his cheeks turning red. He looked at Emma and then across to Maria and John.

"Well, there might be a bit more to the story but officially she's just helping me out. I would like to get the next couple of weeks out of the way before we say anything. I hope you two can keep that promise."

They all raised their glasses and said cheers. The rest of the evening went with them discussing what they all would like to do once the whole Bank issue was over. They all agreed that a night out would be one of the first things on the list.

It had gone past midnight by the time Ben and Emma were getting into bed. And although Ben had enjoyed the evening, he was very tired now and ready for bed. Before turning off the light he gave her a kiss and said 'I love you'. Emma couldn't quite believe what she had just heard. What he had just said sounded like it came from the heart and he really meant it. *He is getting better by the day* she thought and fell asleep.

Monday morning Ben arranged with Mr. Anderson's secretary that he could see them Wednesday morning at ten. Now he just needed John's help to gather all the relevant paperwork so he could drop it off later. He was heading into town with his dad to get some paint for the room he was going to do up in his house. They had talked about what color to choose and decided that a very light blue one would be good.

Ben had a quick look at the calendar: there was no ride Wednesday morning so he quickly put a line through it. He needed John to come with him to see Mr. Anderson as John was much more knowledgeable on the finance side of things than him.

Helen came into the office.

"Wanna come outside for a coffee?"

"Yeah, can do. Be there in a minute."

"Okay I'll get your father to get some chairs."

Bill got sent to get some chairs so they could enjoy the weather while the two patients went for a little walk. Helen started talking about how lovely it was that John had come home and was willing to help out.

"It would be so nice if he lived a bit closer to us. Don't you think? You two seem to be getting on very well."

Ben couldn't deny that but in terms of John moving home, well, that had to be for John to tell them, not him.

"Yeah, it was lucky he could and yes, we seem to be doing well together. Maybe this will get him thinking, you never know." He wouldn't say any more on that.

They returned to the front of the house again and Bill had managed to find three chairs for them to sit on.

"Who'd like a coffee?" Helen looked at both Bill and Ben who both nodded.

"I'll give you a hand." But before Ben could get out of the chair Helen had stopped him.

"No, you stay right there. I'm not having you lifting anything. Your father can come and help me." She gave Bill a firm look.

Ben was feeling so good that he had forgotten about the 'no lifting' and he realized that it was probably going to be very difficult for him to stick to the rules.

As they were sat there enjoying their coffee, Helen started to talk about Emma: how lovely she was and that it was very good of her to stay with him at the house so he wasn't on his own. Ben couldn't quite gauge whether it was Helen fishing for information, or she just generally thought that Emma was that loyal a worker but he had a suspicion that it was fishing, and he wasn't going to bite, not yet anyway. So instead of letting on his feelings for Emma, he told them that he had spoken to Emma's father and that he was offering his help and advice with their meeting with the Bank.

"That'll cost you, son," it was the first time Bill had spoken whilst they had sat there.

"In fact, not a lot as we have always treated Emma so well. That was his words to me earlier today." Ben didn't say anything about the chat he had had with Mr. Anderson Saturday evening.

"That's very kind of him." Helen offered them both cookies.

"Yeah, let's just hope he can help us enough. He will need some paperwork which I will get John to sort out and we can drop it in when we head in to get the paint later." Ben was rather looking forward to get into town, it would be a welcome distraction for him. This staying at home wasn't doing him any good, his body felt restless.

The sun was quite hot and, in the end, they had to retreat indoors.

"Hey dad, why don't I go with you for a drive and we can check out the land tomorrow?"

"Sure thing, son." Bill looked up from the paper he was reading.

"That's a good idea," Helen popped her head in. "But no lifting gates or anything like that for you, son."

"I promise."

At lunch, Ben told John about the meeting he had arranged and that Mr. Anderson would like to have a look at the paperwork beforehand.

"Dad and I are heading to town to get some paint, we could drop it off this afternoon."

"Great. Won't take long as I kind of sorted it already," John headed into the office and returned with a folder.

"Where exactly is your father's office, Emma?" Ben was fairly sure he knew but wanted to be safe.

"Just around the corner from Maria's shop. It's very easy to find." She had put her hand on his leg under the table and Ben had to be very strong not to give any hint about his feelings for her. He had to admit it was getting more and more difficult to not show anything. *Only another two weeks and a bit*, he thought.

So, in order to get to Mr. Anderson's office, they had to drive past Maria's shop and then turn right. Ben couldn't help glancing across to the other side as they passed the tourist shop. There it was, the biggest building on the main street, overlooking all the others. It sent shivers down his spine and made him feel sick. He had really come to hate that place.

Bill managed to park right outside Mr. Anderson's office and Ben insisted that he should drop the folder in. He was met by a very kind lady at the reception who promised him that she would hand it to Mr. Anderson straight away. Part of Ben felt really relieved that he had done it; he had reached out for help and now it was just a question of hoping that Mr. Anderson could help them.

Emma and John had a full day with the horses the following day. Bill kept his promise; he took Ben for a drive around on their land. Ben thought they were just going to check cattle but it turned into a full morning where Bill explained everything about all the corners of the land they owned and a bit about the neighbors. Everything was covered from good to failed crops over the years, weather issues, etc. to the point that Ben completely lost track of time. They returned home late for lunch, the others had been and gone again but Helen hadn't had hers. As they sat there, the three of them, Ben thanked his father for the tour.

"That was some tour, dad."

"Yeah, your mom and I had a long talk with John last night. We've been thinking a lot over what to do in light of what has been going on. And before you say anything, this was partly John's idea just so you know that he is fully in on it."

Ben felt his stomach tightening up and his mind had started running slightly out of control. *What had John suggested?*

"And what exactly did you come up with?" This came out a bit harder than he intended.

"You have nothing to worry about, son. First, the ranch will be handed to you once we've sorted out the issue with the

Bank. John told us, and I believe he told you as well, that he will pay the outstanding amount if no other solutions come up but he is pretty sure that with Mr. Anderson's help that won't be needed. He said he had had some advice from his boss in New York."

"Okay..." Ben wasn't sure what to say and was wondering what was coming next.

"He also said, which has if I may say so made your mother very happy, that he is relocating here, well, not here on the ranch but he plans to move in with Maria which has come as a big surprise for us." Bill was holding Helen's hand and they were looking at each other before turning their faces to Ben.

Ah, so John had told them of his plans.

"I knew he was thinking of coming home but didn't know where he planned to live." He hoped that he had sounded convincing enough.

Bill looked at Helen again who nodded as if to say 'go on'.

"Your mother and I will stay here but only as long as you want us here. When you get married or have a partner it will be our pleasure to hand the house to you." They were both looking at him as if they expected him to tell them something.

Ben was trying to take all that in even though he had known all along that one day this would happen. But no matter how much you know that something is going to take place one day in the future, when it happens it comes as a surprise. On top of that he had to be careful not to say too much; it would be so easy to tell them everything but what if it didn't work out?

"Thank you." It was all he could manage.

"Ben, I know that one day you will raise your own family in this house," Helen had taken his hand. "You're a very loving young man and you will find your partner in life maybe sooner than you think."

"I know, mom, but right now I have other things to take care of." He tried not to sound too hard and decided that it was time for him to get some fresh air.

"I think I'll go for a little walk, if you don't mind."

"That's fine. We know you have a lot to think about."

Ben got up and headed outside. He needed to be alone to think it all through. It wasn't really new to him but it had suddenly become a reality.

"There you are." Ben turned his head and saw Emma come walking across to him. He was sat at his favorite spot looking out across the land to the mountains in the background.

"Back safely then?" he smiled and took her hand as she sat down next to him.

"Yeah, no problem. What're you thinking of?"

He told her about the trip around and the talk afterwards.

"That's great news, Ben. John did warn me that he had told them about his plans."

"Well, I think my parents might be thinking the same about us. The look, especially my mother had on her face when they spoke about me finding a partner. I didn't let on what's going on as I or we have more important things to focus on at the moment."

"That's absolutely fine, Ben, and it'll all be fine, trust me." They sat for a while just looking at the mountains. Ben had felt it was safe enough to put his arm around Emma. There was no way his parents would be coming out here looking for him.

Later when Emma was helping Helen clean up after dinner, she noticed how happy Helen looked. "I take it you're overjoyed with John moving back here."

"Yeah, it warms my heart. Now I just need Ben to be happy as well." Emma could feel the look and knew she had to be careful what she said.

"I'm pretty sure that Ben will get there one day but he's got a lot on his plate at the moment and you know that he doesn't do well with too much pressure." Emma tried her best to play it down a bit and she suddenly realized what Ben was up against.

{ 18 }

Ben and Emma had headed back to his place after dinner and were sat watching TV or more to the point Emma was as Ben had fallen asleep again. There was a knock on the door and John appeared.

"Hope you don't mind me coming down but I have just had a chat with Pearson, the guy that is building the website. He is keen to know what we think and if there is any more that is needed. Thought we could have a quick look at it together if you don't mind."

"Not a problem. I haven't seen it yet but from what Ben says it looks pretty good. Would you like a beer?" Emma had got up and was heading for the fridge in anticipation of a yes. For Ben's comfort they all sat on the couch with Ben in the middle and the laptop on his knees.

"This is looking great, John. How easy is it to operate?" Emma looked at John.

"Very straight forward. The day-to-day thing is so easy. All you'll have to deal with is emails. In terms of date changes, price changes and things like that I can do, or you and Ben can learn it. If you want to add more things, we just get hold of Pearson to do that."

"Well, brother, you make it sound very easy." Ben wasn't convinced that he would be able to do it, he hadn't really done a lot on computers as it had never had his interest.

"In terms of the website, you will soon get the hang of it, I'm very confident about that. And in terms of the Bank matter, well, I feel pretty confident about that too. It's all going to be fine. Maria has had a lot of good feedback on the brochure and you have had more bookings on the back of that. I have one more thing that you could do and that would be to have a new sign up by the road about Day Rides. Now I'm going to head back up to the house and get some sleep. You should get some as well and try not to worry about it."

And much to Ben's surprise he did have a reasonably good night's sleep. The discomfort from the operation had almost gone, he no longer needed painkillers.

So, the day had arrived and Ben was feeling rather nervous about it. Not really sure if it was because he would learn whether they had a chance against the Bank or whether it was because it was Emma's dad. John was driving them in as Ben still wasn't allowed to drive and not a lot was said in the car.

At Mr. Anderson's office, they were met by the same nice lady Ben had seen two days earlier. She told them to take a seat and that Mr. Anderson would be with them shortly. Ben looked around: it was a very nice place, there were pot plants, comfortable chairs to sit in and even some magazines to look at if you felt the need to distract yourself from whatever was on your mind. There were a couple of doors of which one said Mr. Anderson and some letter which Ben had no idea what it meant and another which he couldn't see what the name was but it clearly meant that there was more than one person working here. The phone kept ringing and a couple of people came in. Ben didn't know them and they didn't seem to know Ben either which he was happy with. He wouldn't exactly like to have word going around town that he had been seen at the lawyer's office.

Mr. Anderson's door opened and he came out to greet them.

"Morning, you two. What a lovely day we have. Come on in." As they walked in, he carried on.

"Did you have a good evening the other night? I haven't had a chance to catch up with Emma yet."

The door was closed behind them.

"Yeah, it was nice." Ben managed not to sound too nervous. "And sorry she's been too busy especially with me not being able to do anything."

"How are you getting on? I know you're probably very frustrated not being able to do what you normally do but you'll get back to it. Make the most of having your brother here, it won't hurt him doing some proper work," he laughed and then turned to John.

"So, when are you planning on going back to New York, young man?"

"Well, actually I'm not. I'm relocating here and to start with, I'll continue working for the company from here with a monthly trip back but hope they either open up a branch here or I build up a client base and start on my own."

"Music to my ears, son, we could do with a few of your type here to bring us into the modern world. Let me know if I can help you in any way." He shuffled a few papers around.

"Now, to this minor thing with the Bank. You'll be pleased

to know that I have no doubt in that you will continue with the ranch. Looking through this contract, there are a few things that the Bank hasn't fulfilled and I'll be happy to take this all the way if needed, I just need your permission."

He went on to explain about the errors in the contract or more the things the Bank had conveniently forgotten to let them know about. The mortgage was set up with a flexible interest rate but had never changed even when the rates had gone down. There was also a bit in there about the Bank offering a review if they had better deals, etc.

"So that's that. In terms of going forward with the business, what've you been thinking?"

Now it was John's turn and he explained about the brochure, website and then took out the business plan he had drawn up.

"This is excellent work, boys. You've really shown an effort to turn this around and by the sound of it, you've already seen results. Very good work." Mr. Anderson was looking through it all and clearly looked very happy. "Well, so how do we go from here? That's the next question. I propose that I put a letter together for you in which we highlight the various issues plus your plan for the future. I'll keep a low profile, make it out that it is coming from you. This gives the Bank a chance to correct themselves which I suspect they won't in which case we'll hit harder."

"Sounds like a plan." John looked at Ben and then back to Mr. Anderson. "Will you email me the letter before it goes just so I have an idea what it says? Oh, and just to let you know, I had a long talk with mom and dad and they have decided to hand the ranch on to Ben once this is all over. We will have to sort all that out afterwards."

"That is excellent news, Ben. Congratulations and of course, I will email you the letter, John. Now what you probably will get is a lot of calls or letters from them and even a visit. Please keep me in the loop and should it get too much, I'll be ready to step in." He then turned his attention to Ben.

"Son, I know Emma says you're worried about all this and rightly so but I'm pretty sure it'll all be fine. You might have a couple of weeks where you'll be tested in terms of patience but you will be stronger at the end of it, I'll promise you that."

"Okay... Tested in what way?"

"Oh, I'm pretty sure Mr. Miles will be in contact with you both by letter but also in person. He'll try and tell you that they've done everything they could etc. Don't say anything; just let me know what he says, and we'll deal with it."

Ben couldn't help thinking of the nightmare he had had about Mr. Miles and was beginning to feel slightly uncomfortable.

"You're a fine, young and hardworking man, Ben, who deserves to be treated better than what they have done. I'm very proud of my daughter's choice of man." Mr. Anderson got up.

Ben couldn't quite believe what he had just heard. *What did he just say?* He didn't have time to think about it as they all shook hands and soon him and John were heading for the car.

On the way home, John was smiling.

"I'd say that you have been accepted in the family." He looked at Ben who was very quiet.

He was trying to understand it all. How much exactly had Emma told her parents about him and their relationship? He decided that he had to speak to her later about it. And why should he worry? Her father had just told him that he was good enough for their daughter. What did all that mean?

"What do you think the Bank is going to do? I mean do we need to warn mom and dad? And why can't we just walk in, show them what we have and take it from there?"

"It isn't that straight forward, Ben. Yes, in some way we could but it would only mean that they can continue with their dirty tricks. What Mr. Anderson is trying to do is to build a case that will end with the manager being removed. Not many people or companies have the energy and connections to put up the fight at this stage. We're lucky that we have Mr. Anderson and hopefully this will lead to a better Bank."

Ben could kind of see what John was saying but just wished that he wasn't the guinea pig.

"What exactly have you told your parents about us?" They were sat watching TV and Ben had finally picked up the courage to ask her. It was still playing on his mind and he couldn't quite work out what to make of it.

"What do you mean?" Emma looked at him with confusion.

"Your father told me today that he was 'very proud of

your choice of man'," he didn't know whether to laugh or be serious.

"Did he say that? Well, I haven't told them anything about us so this is news to me too," she cuddled up to him and Ben had no option but to put his arm around her.

"How does he know then?"

"Look, Ben, I wouldn't worry about it. At least he didn't say he disapproved of you." She laughed. "And I think you'll find that your parents have a feeling too."

"Really?"

"Yep, I'll bet 10 bucks on that if we went to ask them now, they would say yes."

Ben didn't really know what to say to that but when he thought of it, they *were* spending a lot of time together and he had to admit that Emma had a way of putting him in a good mood.

The next few days went without any incidents. Ben managed with his parents' help to tidy up the two spare rooms in his house. There had been a number of boxes stored away in them from his grandparents' time in the house. Each one of them had been checked, some of the things had been thrown out while others had gone back up to the house for Bill to go through at his own pace.

Sunday came and whilst Emma and John took a group out, Ben decided that he would try and go for a little drive. He was desperate to get out and do things. The week ahead wasn't going to be easy and he could feel the tension building in his head.

After a minor argument with his parents over whether he

should or shouldn't drive, he got in the truck. *I will be fine*, he kept saying to himself. He had no plans to go far, just out to his favorite spot by the river. He had also taken his fishing gear with him.

No one was going to disturb him here unless Emma and John decided to take the rides this way but that was highly unlikely as it would be a longer ride and normally only done when they had one ride a day.

As he was sat there watching the water flow by, he started to think of all the things that had happened over the last month or so. It was as if someone had grabbed the jar they were in – one of those you have at Christmas that you shake and snowflakes get stirred up and then slowly fall down. He couldn't remember what they were called. The question was how was it all going to fall down. What direction would it take? How could everyone be so sure that it would all be okay?

Right now, Ben couldn't see past the end of the following week. He kept getting the picture of Mr. Miles in his head, he could almost see the joy in his eyes when he would tell them that it was over. And then what? What was going to happen to him and to his parents? What was he going to do? What kind of life could he offer Emma? She was everything he wanted, she made him feel so much better, there was no doubt in that, but would it be fair on her? At the end of it all, he would be left with nothing at the end of the week, nowhere to live and not a penny to his name.

He could feel the tears running down his face. He had

fallen into the trap again but this time it was him having to end it.

He had no idea what the time was when his phone went ping. A text from Emma asking if he was okay. He thought for a while and just replied 'yes'. He couldn't end things over the phone, he wouldn't do that to her. No, he had to face her and explain why – or was there another way out of it? He looked at the water.

Back at the house John and Emma had returned from their afternoon ride and there was still no sign of Ben. Both Helen and Bill had been concerned at lunch time but John had said that Ben was probably fishing and had forgotten the time. He will get back soon.

"Did you get a reply from him, Emma?" Helen was beginning to look a bit upset.

"Yeah, he said he was fine. I'll try and call him," she headed out with John right behind her.

"What was his reply, Emma?" John had a feeling that Emma was covering something.

"I asked if he was okay and this was the reply I had," she showed him the text.

"Hmm," John was trying to work out what to do next but before he could say anything Emma said, "I think I know where he is."

They both decided that it probably would be a good idea to check it out. Not a lot was said on the way and as they got closer to the river, they saw the truck. Emma had been right. She parked her car a bit behind and as they got out, Emma was relieved to see Ben sat there with his back to them looking out over the water. He wasn't fishing. Emma looked at John and they decided both to head down to him.

"Hey, what are you doing out here?" Emma started to talk a bit before they got to him to make him aware that they were there. "Everybody's wondering where you are," she went and sat down next to him. John sat on the other side. It was clear to them both that Ben had been crying. Emma went to put her arm around him to comfort him but Ben just sat there staring out on the river.

"It's all over," he said.

"Sorry, what's over?" Emma looked at him and then to John as if to say *this is bad.*

"Ben, what's over? What are you talking about?" John looked at him.

"All of it. The ranch, me and Emma, everything..."

"Where has all this come from?" John finally realized how big a burden this whole thing must have been for Ben.

"Ben, look at me." Emma had tears in her eyes. "No matter what happens this coming week, I will always be by your side. Don't you ever doubt that. I don't care if we have to live in a trailer, I still love you." She had got hold of his hand.

"Ben, I know that you've been under a lot of pressure lately but I can assure you that you're going nowhere. By the end of the week, you'll still be here running this place. Remember you have a backup plan – me. If you want me to, I can go and pay it tomorrow but I'd like to set things straight with the Bank as I feel they have tricked you, mom and dad."

Ben could feel he was getting tearful again. All his plans about ending things with Emma – he realized that there was no way he could do it. He wasn't strong enough to do that. For years he had not allowed himself to have any kind of feeling for anyone and now that he had it, he just couldn't let it go.

"Are you really sure you want to stay with me if I have nothing?" He looked straight into Emma's eyes and all she did was bend over and kiss him.

"I will never leave you, Ben."

John was beginning to get quite emotional too and was trying hard to keep his head straight.

"Hey guys, why don't I take the truck back and leave you two to come home when you're ready? But, first, Ben. Please don't think you will lose anything this week. I know it's hard on you because you can't do anything and I know things might get a bit hairy but we will get through it. I have full confidence in Mr. Anderson."

"I know but I can't help it. I feel completely left out at the moment; not being able to do anything is really hard."

"I realize that but you will come out as a stronger man at the other end. Trust me. Now I'll leave you two here and head back to calm mom down. She's worried about you."

"Thanks, John." Ben got up and gave his brother a big brother hug. "Keys in the truck and please don't tell them about this."

"I won't. As far as they know, you've had a bad day fishing – not caught a single one." John winked and headed home.

Emma had stayed sat down thinking about what had happened. Deep down she had feared the worst when he hadn't replied to her messages. Ben came and joined her again and took her hand.

"I'm really sorry," he said with tears in his eyes.

"Ben." Emma looked him straight in the eyes, "I love you; I always have and always will no matter what happens this coming week. Do you understand that?"

"Yes, I do but if I lose everything, I can't expect you to give up everything for me. What would your parents think?"

"They love you, Ben, and my dad is pretty certain that you'll be walking away as a winner by the end of the week."

He bent over, wrapped his arms around her and kissed her. They didn't move for a while. In the end, Emma said,

"Come on, let me take you home. I don't want you to get too cold."

They went straight to his house and while Ben had a shower, Emma went to let the others know that he was fine but had realized he had overdone it a bit so he was going to bed early. John walked back with Emma. It was going to be a hard week for them all but in particular Ben and he had an idea he wanted to run by her.

Ben was sat on the couch when they walked in. *He looks mentally drained,* John thought.

"What would you say to try and sit on a horse tomorrow?" Ben immediately perked up and John knew it would be the right thing to do.

"Am I allowed to?" Ben looked at Emma who smiled.

"I think it'd be good for you. Why don't we try tomorrow after the ride?"

Ben hadn't had any discomfort lately and as long as he

wasn't going to lift the saddle up, he would probably be fine although the getting on could be tricky he thought. They agreed that when John and Emma were back from a ride in the afternoon, Ben would come up and they would try it out.

Ben was feeling a little bit nervous which he found strange. He who had ridden all his life. In order to make it as easy as possible for Ben and without putting too much strain on the scar tissue they decided to use the stand that was there for customers who found it difficult to get on a horse from the ground. It meant that he didn't have to bend too much. It felt a little tight getting on but once in the saddle he was fine. Emma suggested that they did a little ten-minute ride to see if he had any discomfort. The only issue he really had was the slight discomfort getting on and off; otherwise, he felt really good. There were no rides the next morning and between them they decided that he and Emma would go for a little ride.

The following day Ben had no issues in terms of having sat on a horse the day before and they decided that a gentle ride out to the cattle would be good for him as long as Emma was the one that got on and off when needed. It felt so good being back in the saddle and Ben couldn't stop talking about it over lunch.

Ben watched John with a big smile on his face and Emma ride out with a group after lunch before heading into town. It filled him with joy seeing them heading up the hill and on to the plains above and he was pretty sure that his brother was enjoying it.

Ben made a phone call and headed into town. Maria was waiting for him with a cup of coffee.

"Good to see you out and about, Ben, and I hear you've even been back on the horse. Make sure you don't rush it," she gave him a hug. "Now what is it you'd like me to help you with?" She had walked him into their little staff room.

Ben felt a little nervous about it and he wanted her to promise him that she wouldn't say anything to anyone – not even John. He quickly filled her in about the meeting with Mr. Anderson, his comment about him and then went on to ask her for some help.

"Fantastic news. I'm so proud of you, Ben, and don't worry my lips are sealed. Why don't we go and have a look now?"

Maria told her assistant that she was going out for a while and they headed out on to the busy main street. Ben couldn't help having a look across the road and it sent shivers down his spine. Maria spotted it and tugged her arm into his.

"Don't you worry about them, Ben, they will be the ones that are sorry come Friday. No doubt about it."

"I don't understand how y'all can be so optimistic about it. Yes, I know what Mr. Anderson has told me but still. Why do I find it so difficult?"

"Ben, it's all about the power of positive thinking. Some of us find it very natural to stay positive, others have to work at it. I know you've been through your fair share of bad news and that doesn't make it easier to try and be positive but trust me, you'll feel so much better."

"How do you mean?" Ben was a little puzzled by this.

"Well, instead of thinking that it's all going to end on Friday, try thinking that you'll come out as the winner in this. So, every time they either call or send a letter regarding Friday, you just keep telling yourself that you'll win. I know it's going to be hard and at times you'll have to work very hard to try and say it but I know you can."

"Okay, I'll give it a shot." Ben thought to himself that he couldn't really lose anything by trying and if it could help calm his nerves, so much the better.

They had reached the place and headed in.

After dinner Ben stayed up at the house for a bit. Emma had to go home and sort something out but had made sure that Ben was happy to be on his own overnight.

It turned out to be a lovely evening with the four of them. They had all been taking turns to tell some of their memories from years gone by on the ranch. Ben had even ventured to talk about what he would like to do with the place. For instance, the house could do with a coat of paint and a few updates but also a few things he would like to add into the activities for their customers.

John had heard from Maria that she had given him a bit of a talk on how to cope with the week and for now that seemed to work. When he had asked Maria what Ben was in town for, she just said he felt like having a chat with an old friend and he was not to ask questions on it. She came up with a line about how this was all part of Ben trying to cope with it all. Fair enough; John didn't think more about it.

By the time Ben headed back to his house, it was late and it wasn't until he opened the door that it hit him that he was to spend the night alone. Luckily, he was rather tired after the day's events and decided to head straight for bed but first he wanted to just have another look at it.

Was it the right thing to do? Well, he had talked it through with Maria and that had helped him make up his mind. Now he just needed to get the Bank issue out of the way. He thought about what Maria had said about positive thinking.

The alarm went off and Ben put his arm out to turn it off then went to turn around to see Emma. Only then did he remember that she had stayed at her parents' last night. His body felt tired like he had been working very hard all night. Surely it wasn't the ride yesterday that had done that to him, he wasn't aching anywhere. *Very odd*, he thought and got out of bed.

{ 19 }

As he walked up to the house, he spotted his mom out with her hens.

"Morning, mom. Are you glad to be back with your hens?"

"Oh, morning, Ben. Yeah, nice to be able to do a bit again. Sleep okay?"

"Yeah, but must have been busy in my dream as I feel like I've done a full day's work already. Maybe it's a sign that I need to get on and do a bit," he held the door for her as she came up the few steps.

"I'll have your breakfast ready in a minute," she rushed into the kitchen.

Not long after, Emma's car appeared and Emma herself in her usual style walked into the kitchen with a smile on her face.

"Morning, everyone! All okay?" She looked at Ben and tried her best not to show how much she had missed him. As per normal she went and sat down next to him, grabbed his hand under the table and gave it a squeeze. They all started to tell her about the stories they had heard the night before. The phone rang and Ben said he would take it.

"Hello. Jackson Ranch here."

"Hello, Mr. Jackson. Mr. Miles here." Ben froze when he heard the voice.

"How can I help you." He managed to control himself whilst thinking how he dared to ring them.

"I just thought I'd remind you that I'll be coming out on Friday so I hope you'll have the cash sorted out."

"Looking forward to see you. Sorry, gotta run as we're busy here." He put the phone down and then realized he was shaking. His hands were sweating and his head was spinning. How rude was that? Ben hadn't spotted that John and Emma had come into the room. They had heard most of the conversation as Ben had almost shouted into the phone.

"I assume that was our Bank manager," John looked at Ben.

"What did he say, Ben?" Emma had grabbed hold of Ben's hand and got him to sit down.

"He says he will see us on Friday and hopes we have the cash ready for him." Ben was staring out into the room.

"Well, he might be in for a bit of a surprise then," John went to get the phone but before he could dial the number Ben looked at him and said:

"Wait, I'd like to make that call, if you don't mind." Emma and John looked at each other and John handed the phone to Ben.

"Emma, what's your father's number?" Ben remembered what Maria had told him the day before and took a deep breath. "I'll be so glad when we see the back of this man," he said and dialed the number. A lady answered and Ben asked to speak to Mr. Anderson as soon as possible.

"One moment. I'll put you through."

The next thing he heard was, "Hello, Ben. How are you

doing?" For a second, Ben wasn't sure what to say but then relayed the experience he had just had. "Right, I see; he is up to his dirty tricks again. Well, this will be his last one I feel. Don't worry, Ben, I'll make a few calls and I'll come out on Friday to meet him. Did he say any time?"

Ben couldn't remember a time being mentioned.

"Not to worry; I'll be with you in the morning. In the meantime, try not to worry about it."

"Thank you, Mr. Anderson. We look forward to see you."

The phone call had rather put a bit of a damper on the breakfast mood. *This is going to be a long week if we don't do something*, John thought.

"This will all sort itself out, trust me. Now how many on the rides today and have we got any booked for Friday?" John looked at his mother and she went to get the book.

"A few for this afternoon, two groups tomorrow and so far, Friday is clear."

"Good. I suggest that we keep Friday clear. Ben, do you think you'll be fit enough to check cattle with Emma? I have something I need to do in town but will be back for this afternoon. Dad, you okay to take mom for her check up at the hospital?"

Yes, Helen was due to go and have a follow up appointment at the hospital. Ben had completely forgotten all about that.

"Yeah, a ride would do me good, I think," he looked at Emma and smiled.

"Good. And Emma, would you like to spend Friday evening at the rodeo show with us? We can all go and celebrate together. Pretty sure Maria would love to come along too."

"Yes, that would be fun."

"Mom, dad, would you like to come as well?"

Helen looked at Bill. It had been years since they had been but why not?

"Even better. I'll buy the tickets. It will be my way of saying thank you for still loving me even though I haven't been very good at staying in touch."

Ben was trying to work out what John was up to. Why would he do this? He didn't have time to dwell on it for too long as Emma was already on her way out of the door.

"Are you coming or not?" she gave him a smile.

"On my way." Ben turned to John and gave him a look. "What are you up to, brother?" But John just gave him a smile and said to enjoy himself.

Emma was more than halfway to the yard when Ben caught up with her. As soon as they were out of sight from the house, he put his arms around her and gave her a big hug, his scar reminding him about not lifting her.

"God, I've missed you," he kept hold of her like she was the thing he was hanging on to avoid drowning.

"I don't know what I would do without you, Emma. And please tell me you'll stay tonight?"

"Yes, I'll stay."

Emma got the horses ready as Ben couldn't lift the saddles up and over yet. It didn't take long and soon they were on the way. *This was definitely the best medicine,* Ben thought as they left the ranch behind them. There was no rush and Ben suggested that they rode down by the river but he had to promise Emma that he wouldn't get off the horse. It wasn't quite the same staying on, there was something about the half sitting half lying on the riverbank. He was looking around to see if there was anything he could use to stand on for next time he would come out here.

"So, are you okay with Friday?" Emma broke the silence.

He looked at her; her eyes were so beautiful; she had her hair in a ponytail underneath the hat. He really loved that long slightly wavy blonde hair. How come he had never really taken any notice of it before?

"Sorry, what was that?"

"I was talking about Friday. Are you okay with it?" She looked at him thinking that he was acting a bit strange.

"Yeah, I think I'll be fine. I had a chat with Maria yesterday and she told me all about how I should try and think positive and all that. I have to admit that I find it very difficult at times like this morning but there was something in what your dad said to me or maybe it was the way he said it that I feel more secure about it now. And the fact that he'll be here is making me feel even better."

"Ben, I'm proud of you. You have really worked very hard even when life hasn't been that easy for you." She had lined up her horse next to his so she could hold his hand.

"Emma, if you had a choice of working here or somewhere else, what would you choose?"

"Here definitely. I love this place, I love you and your family, and I couldn't think of being anywhere else."

It made Ben feel very good and he smiled.

"Why are you asking me this?" She looked at him like he was up to no good.

"Just wondering. We're not always that easy, you know," he gave her a big smile.

"Come on; we better head home before I jump off."

They had actually been gone for quite a while but it didn't matter as there was no one else at home.

Both John, Bill and Helen returned by lunch. Helen's check-up had gone well despite the stress in the morning and she was signed off from the hospital for now but told to take it easy and slow down a bit. John looked like he had been shopping, judging by the bags he was holding.

"Going somewhere?" Ben was teasing him.

"Well, I thought that if we're going to a rodeo show I better have some clothes that would be appropriate for it. Don't you think?"

He had a point there. It was a limited wardrobe John had at the moment as most of his stuff was still in New York. Not that any of that would have been suitable for a rodeo show.

Somehow the rest of the day and the following day went without Ben thinking too much about the upcoming Friday. It was like everyone had decided not to talk about it and just get on with things.

As Ben hadn't experienced any discomfort from riding, they decided that he could ride out with Emma on the Thursday afternoon. John had some work calls he needed to make and the group was fairly big. He did however go and help them get ready as Ben still couldn't lift the saddles – it was the up and over he couldn't do yet. As they were riding along

Ben couldn't help thinking that this is the life – riding out with a group of people who are interested in what he and his family did for a living.

Just before they reached the last bit where you get to the edge of the plain, he couldn't help but to stop and point out the view. From here you had a view of the ranch and most of the land they farmed. He was fighting hard not to think of what could happen tomorrow but if they had to move, this would be one of the spots he would miss most. Luckily, he got disrupted by a comment from one of the participants on the ride before he started to go too far in his negative thought.

"Thank you so much for this ride and what a lovely place you live in, Mr. Jackson. I'll definitely come back."

"Thank you and we look forward to see you again," Ben smiled and reminded himself about what Maria had said to him.

Dinner was a little on the quiet side. They had all voted for a BBQ and Maria had come out to join them. If this was going to be the last one, it had to be a special one. That had been Ben's view when he had suggested it. He wasn't the only one that had doubt, both Bill and Helen looked very concerned but John had said it would all be fine and that the subject wasn't to be discussed, ending it with "let's have a nice evening together".

Halfway through dinner, John stood up.

"As you all know, I've been thinking about moving back here for good. Today I had a meeting with my boss and a couple of others and it's now official. I am from now on based in Montana, they've found a small office right next door to your father's, Emma, which will be where I will work from. It starts with immediate effect and Monday morning I have to be there to receive my office furniture etc. So, mom and dad, you'll now be seeing a lot more of me. And Ben, I hope you'll be fit enough to take your job back. Cheers!"

Both Bill and Helen had tears running down their faces and John went around to give them a hug.

"That is some of the best news I've had in a long time. Thank you, John." Helen was holding Bill's hand.

Ben felt so pleased; not only had John made his parents' wishes come true but it also made Ben feel better. Now he knew that his brother wouldn't disappear again. He had come to like having John around.

John then went around to Maria and took her hand.

"Maria, I have known you for a long time now but never really appreciated how much I enjoy spending time with you and how happy you make me. I know this might come as a surprise but I wouldn't like to spend one more day without you." He got down on one knee. "Will you marry me?"

He had taken a ring out of his pocket and was holding her hand.

No one said a thing. You could hear a needle drop and it seemed to go on forever and it had taken everyone by surprise including Maria.

"Yes, of course, I'll marry you!" Maria finally replied and everyone cheered.

Both Helen and Emma wanted to see the ring.

"Congrats, brother. Talk about lightening the mood.

When did you decide to do this?" Ben gave his brother a big hug.

"Thanks, brother. Well, soon after I came back when mom was ill. I don't know, there was just something that made me feel I had found the right one and I don't want to waste any more time. You should take notes here." John gave him a nudge.

"Well, I'm happy for you both."

It had definitely changed the mood of the evening from being a bit on the quiet side to be very joyful and at no point did anyone mention anything about what was going to happen the next day.

It was nearly midnight by the time Ben and Emma made their way down to the house.

"Why do you think John decided to do it tonight? And had he said anything to you?" Ben was still pondering over what had happened.

"It was the first I knew about it, I just think John has realized that he has found what he feels is right for him. They seem very happy together. Don't you think?" Emma was looking at Ben and wondering if he would ever be able to do a similar thing.

"Yeah, maybe you're right. I still think it was a bit of a risk to take. What if she had said no there in front of us all?"

"Well, she didn't and he must have felt very confident about her answer. How do you feel about John being back here permanently and with Maria?"

"So glad. I think my problem was more that I was angry with him for not being here. But I can kind of understand why. It wasn't that he didn't want to but more like he got caught up in work. Have you noticed that he looks a lot more relaxed now?" Emma could only agree. John wasn't drinking the same amount of coffee as when he first arrived and he was spending less time on his phone too.

They had reached the house and Ben opened the door. Emma was very tired and not really up for sitting and talking things through.

"Come, Ben, let's hit the pillows. It's very late and we have another day tomorrow."

Oh yes, didn't they just. Ben found it a bit difficult to fall asleep. He was fighting the negative thoughts in his head and as he laid there watching Emma sleeping, he couldn't help thinking that if he was to propose to her, he would want to do it somewhere where it was just the two of them in case she said no.

He must have fallen asleep at some point as he was woken by Emma telling him to turn the alarm off. He was so confused but then remembered what day it was. *Well, this is it* he thought as he got dressed. Emma didn't say a lot either which was a little unusual for her, she was normally the one that could talk in the mornings. It had been decided the day before that they would all have breakfast together but as it turned out, no one really felt like it.

Ben went for a walk around the barns and the house. He was a bit nervous and found it difficult to sit down.

Meanwhile, Emma was talking to Maria who let on that she had no idea that John was going to propose to her last night.

"I wonder if Ben will ever get to trust someone enough for him to do the same," Emma was looking at the beautiful sparkling ring on Maria's finger.

"He will, I'm pretty sure of that. I think he's feeling a lot better now in terms of relationships. He just got himself tied in knots; let's face it there has been a lot going on here. Don't you think?"

"Yeah, it sure has been some interesting weeks. Still, business seems to be picking up which is good."

Ben came in looking concerned.

"There are a couple of cars coming. Doesn't he feel strong enough to do this on his own?" Ben was getting a little sharp.

"No, that'll be dad." Emma got up and went to Ben. "It's okay. He just sent me a message saying he was on the way and he was bringing someone with him. I have no idea who."

Both Ben and John went out to meet them. And yes, it was Mr. Anderson in one car and three men in another one. Mr. Anderson introduced the three men to Ben and John. The north western area manager for the Bank and two investigators from the head office of the Bank.

"I hear congratulations are in order," Mr. Anderson was looking at John and Maria once they were inside and he turned to his team and explained what had happened – Emma had informed him of the news from the night before.

As they were all sat there having coffee, the area manager asked if it was okay to talk about the business in front of everyone.

"Yes, they are all part of the family," Bill said sharply.

"Thank you. I thought I'd ask first. Now I believe that you've drawn up a business plan," he was looking at Ben.

"Yeah, yes, my brother has," Ben pointed towards John.

"Would you be kind enough to show it to me?"

The manager had turned to face John who was more than happy to run through it. As Ben was sat there listening to it, he felt very proud of his brother and the hours John must have put into making it. He just hoped that they would accept it.

At the end of John's talk, the manager thanked him and looked at him.

"Where did you say you worked again?"

John explained all that and that he was coming back to the area.

"Good to know. I'll remember that..." he was about to go on when a car arrived.

Ben shut up. He had arrived- the moment of truth had come and all he could hope for was that it would turn out the way everyone was telling him, he still wasn't a hundred percent sure it would work. Bill had got up too and was heading to the door.

"Dad, allow me to deal with him, please." Ben had decided that this was one he had to deal with. It was now or never, he felt. He took a deep breath and walked outside, down the few steps and stopped.

Mr. Miles got out of his car, looked around with that weird grin on his face.

"What a lovely morning it is. I see you have guests. Are they here to help?"

Ben wasn't entirely sure what he meant with that but forced himself to stay grounded. "Welcome." He wasn't prepared to shake hands with him; instead, he took a split decision and called John who immediately appeared at the door. "John, could you please tell our guests who has arrived? I think they would like to see."

Ben had no intention of inviting Mr. Miles in; there was no way that man was walking through the doors of the house if he could help it.

Mr. Anderson appeared on the doorstep followed by the three other men.

"Morning, Mr. Miles, you're out and about early today I see."

To Ben's surprise, he watched the color from Mr. Miles' face literally disappear when he saw the others.

The men had come down and were standing next to Ben now.

"Morning, Mr. Miles, I am Mr. Johnson, your North West area manager and these two are Mr. Heath and Mr. Cooper from Head Office. We've already had a meeting here and it's all been taken care of for now. If you'd be kind enough to come with us back to the Bank and for security reasons, you'll be driving with these two gentlemen and I will take your car. Is that all understood?"

Mr. Miles was looking from one to another and didn't look that comfortable about it but well enough to mutter directly to Ben: "You will pay for this. I will make sure you lose everything." There was a really hateful look on his face but before Ben could say anything, Mr. Anderson stepped in.

"Are you threatening my client?" He looked very sternly at Mr. Miles who by now was flanked by the two men from Headquarters.

"This way, and can we have your keys, please," one of them said. Mr. Miles got led to their car.

"I'll follow in a second," Mr. Johnson said and turned to Mr. Anderson and Ben.

"Mr. Jackson, it's been a pleasure to meet you and you will hear from us in due course. Here is a letter explaining what will happen but I can safely tell you that you won't be going anywhere. Mr. Anderson can explain what's in the letter."

He shook hands with both Ben and John and turned to Mr. Anderson.

"Thank you so much for getting in touch with me. I've been waiting for this moment for a while."

"You're welcome," they shook hands and Mr. Johnson left.

Back in the kitchen, Ben was trying to understand what had just happened. He looked at the envelope and then realized that the rest of the family was watching him. No, he couldn't open it so he handed it to Mr. Anderson and asked him to do it.

The letter explained that their mortgage was suspended pending an investigation. They would be kept informed of what was happening. Mr. Johnson was for now their point of contact if they had any issues.

Ben couldn't believe it. So, it was true, they would not lose the ranch or at least not for now.

"So, what does this exactly mean?" Ben looked at Emma's dad.

"Mr. Miles has been under observation for fraud but they needed a clear case to take him out. He was very clever in the way he set things up, something to do with him secretly owning a business that benefited from all the businesses that he took out. When I contacted Mr. Johnson purely because I wasn't happy with the contract, Mr. Johnson was more than pleased. But in order for nothing to go wrong, I couldn't let anyone know, to minimize the risk of Mr. Miles getting hold of what was going on."

"Okay but what about the mortgage?" Ben was still trying to take it all in.

"It is suspended for now. You've definitely been over charged so you might even get some back but it will take a while for it to be sorted. The important thing is that no one is taking anything from you, Ben." Mr. Anderson had put his hand on Ben's shoulder. "You can relax and get on with your life now."

"I hope he goes to hell and rots there. My friend lost her business because of him." It was Maria who voiced her opinion.

"Those are very strong words, Maria, but I'm with you on that one." Helen was looking very serious.

"Now, guys, let's not dwell on Mr. Miles and what will happen to him. Let's celebrate that Jackson Ranch will carry on to the next generation!" John went to the fridge and pulled out a bottle of champagne.

"Mom, do we have some glasses?"

That was it. Ben turned to Emma, threw his arms around her and lifted her off the floor.

"Careful, Ben, your scar."

Ben immediately put her back down.

John had poured the champagne and each of them was now holding a glass.

"Mr. Anderson, would you do the honors?" John looked at him.

"Long live Jackson Ranch!" Everyone raised their glass.

{ 20 }

"Well, I better get back to the office but we'll be keeping in touch," Mr. Anderson was heading for the door.

Now or never, Ben thought and went after him.

"Mr. Anderson, can I speak to you in private please?" He followed him out.

"Wonder what he wanted to talk to him about," Helen was watching from the window. John said that it was probably to do with how much we owe him for his service. His mind was thinking something else but he kept it to himself.

Maria had to get back to work but promised she would be back in time for them to head to the show that evening. Oh yes, they were all going to the rodeo show. Helen looked at Bill.

"Don't know about you but I definitely need a rest before I do anything else. This has been quite a week so far."

Ben finally came back in.

"If you don't need me this morning, I think I'll head into town and have a look at my new office space and I'll have lunch with Maria."

"No problem. Take your time. Emma and I can handle it here and thanks for helping me through this, brother. Don't think I'd have done it without you."

"Well, we'll never know and it doesn't matter. The important thing is that you get to keep this place."

Ben added, “And I get to see more of you now which I am looking forward to.” He went across to John and gave him a big hug.

John could not resist and whispered into Ben’s ear.

“Go for it.” And as he said it he did a small head toss towards Emma and winked at the same time. Ben pretended he had no clue what he was on about.

“Right, Emma, I think we better go and check the cattle. Are you ready?” Ben was heading for the door.

The sooner he could get out of there, the better. He didn’t want to have to answer any more questions and after the events of the day so far, he could really do with some peace and quiet plus fresh air. In other words, a nice gentle ride out to the fields was what he was in need of.

He was feeling a bit lightheaded and couldn’t decide if it was the alcohol or down to a massive weight being lifted off his shoulders. It still hadn’t sunk in but at the same time he was so happy. He could finally see a future ahead of him and that future was looking good. There was just one thing he needed to do now.

They finally reached the field with the cattle. Everything took a bit longer as it was all down to Emma getting the horses tacked up and ready. Ben felt guilty but there was nothing he could do about it.

As they reached the gate Ben’s heart sank when he saw it had been left open. Why was the gate open? And more to the point, where were all his cattle? Emma got off her horse to check the gate. It wasn’t broken. She then took a close look at the road but there was no evidence of hoof prints which was a good sign, as it would indicate that the cattle were still in there somewhere. Emma got back on after closing the gate behind them.

"Which direction do you think we should head?" She looked at Ben.

This was a big field which could take time. Normally it wouldn't worry her but the fact that the gate was open meant that there was a chance that they wouldn't be here at all. The sooner they could establish their whereabouts, the sooner Ben and she could relax.

"Let's head over to the right and down toward the river where the trees are. It's very warm today so they might have gone for a bit of shelter." Ben was trying to stay calm and not think the worst.

Of all days why did it have to be today? He thought. It didn't take them long to locate the cattle. Ben's thinking had turned out to be right. What a relief. As they got closer, Ben had a good look at them. There were too many to count them all but the fact that they were all together and looked very relaxed was a good sign. The only way to find out if any was missing would be to run them through a crush system and do a head count which would involve a lot of work and definitely not something for a Friday afternoon. The gate had most likely been left open by someone who had decided to camp overnight. It happened from time to time that they would get walkers that did that. Ben had heard stories from other parts of Montana where cattle had been let off fields or fences been broken. It often had to do with neighboring ranches being at war with each other over something. Ben wasn't aware of any issues in the area here and he got on well with his neighbors.

Now that they had located the cattle, they decided to head down to the river and this time Ben got off.

"What are you doing, Ben? How're you going to get back on?" Emma looked at him and couldn't help wondering what he was up to.

"I'll work something out. Now please come and join me." He had taken the reins from both horses and once Emma was off, he parked them up under the tree. Then he walked across to her, took her hand and led her down to the bank of the river.

He had his arm around Emma's shoulders and his head resting on hers. *Now or never,* he thought to himself as they were stood there watching the river. *You can do this man, it's not that difficult.* He took a deep breath, pulled her away a bit and took her hands. Emma looked at him.

"What's up with you? You're acting all weird," she smiled at him.

"Emma, we've known each other for longer than I can remember and you've always been very good to me and my family. You were there when I was feeling down. You're the only one I know that I can fully trust. These last few weeks have shown me that. I, on the other hand, have been blind as a bat until mom fell ill a few weeks ago, maybe I knew it but wouldn't let it in, I don't know. But what I do know now is that I love you more than you can even imagine and I can't even start to think what life would be without you by my side. I know I haven't been easy to deal with but then there has been a lot of things going on and you have stayed here and held my hand when needed. So, Emma Jane Anderson," Ben let go of her hands, dropped down on one knee, pulled out a box from his pocket and opened it, "will you marry me?"

Emma had tears running down her face "Yes, yes, yes, Ben! Of course, I will marry you!" Ben got back up and let the ring slide on to her finger. Perfect fit. Emma threw her arms around him and kissed him. Nothing was said; they stood there with their arms around each other and with happy tears running down their faces. He had done it and she had said yes. Ben had never felt so happy in his life.

"The ring is so beautiful, Ben, and it fits!" Emma kept looking at it and then looking at Ben.

"How did you know what size to get?"

"I had a little help from a friend, a friend I forgot I had."

"Do you mean Maria?" Ben nodded and told her about his visit to town the other day. Emma started to laugh.

"What's so funny about that?" Ben looked at her.

"I asked Maria this morning if she had any idea that John was going to propose to her last night and she said no. And then I said that I wondered whether you would ever do such a thing to which Maria said she was pretty sure you would do it one day. She never let on that she knew."

Ben smiled, "Well, we were best friends back in the day and still are after all these years apart."

"How close?" It came out slightly wrong and Emma regretted asking the question straight away. "Sorry for asking that."

"That's alright. Maria and I were close friends but never more than that. Not once have I ever kissed her or thought of her as a girlfriend. I hope you believe me."

"Yes, I do," she cuddled into him.

"Does anyone else know what you've been up to or are we going home to spring another surprise on everyone?"

"The only other one who knows is your father. That was what I spoke to him about before he left earlier today."

"Really?" Emma sat up. "What did he say?"

"Well, he welcomed me to the family and said it was about time we got this sorted."

"One more question. How are we going to tell the family?"

"Not sure; I didn't think of that part. All I thought was that I wanted to be alone with you when I did it. I wanted it to be a special moment between you and me. I hope you don't mind."

"Not at all. I would have said yes wherever you had asked but this was perfect." She gave him another kiss. "Tell you what. Why don't we take a picture of the ring and send it to the family?"

"That's a good idea," Ben got his phone out and took a picture of Emma's hand with the ring. Then he typed 'She said yes' and sent it to his parents, John and Maria. Emma sent one to her parents with a note saying 'He did it'. It didn't take long for the replies to come in.

Eventually they decided they better head back; after all, they were going out that evening. Ben managed to get back on the horse by standing on a big rock right down by the water and they headed home holding hands all the way whilst talking about what they would do to the ranch when it became theirs.

But first there was a wedding to plan. They were both keen not to wait too long. After all that they had been through they deserved to have some happiness. And as long as it wasn't going to be too big, it shouldn't be that difficult to do. Talking of when, they both said September at the same time. The question then was what John and Maria had planned, if anything.

After a short pause Emma said, "What would you say to a double wedding?"

Ben thought about it. It was something that hadn't crossed his mind at all. There were pros and cons. He wanted the day to be special for him and Emma but at the same time it would be silly having two weddings a short time apart so why not make the day special for all four of them?

"It would be okay with me. What do you think?"

"I personally think it would be a really special day if we did a double wedding here. And especially after what has happened the last few weeks."

Ben couldn't agree more and they decided to ask Maria and John and let them make the decision.

Once back at the yard they quickly got the horses sorted and started to head back to Ben's place to get changed but were spotted from the farm house and called up.

Helen was over the moon and congratulated Ben. To Emma she said, "Now I can call you my daughter."

Even Bill was very pleased.

"Who would have thought the day would turn out to this? Well done, son. I'm proud of you."

Helen wanted to see the ring and then started asking Ben all sorts of question like when he got it, had anybody helped him and when he had decided today was going to be the day. Ben explained he had a little help with the ring and that he had decided the day he bought the ring that he would do it today.

"I think I can safely say that I was a little more prepared than John on this one." As they were stood there admiring Emma's ring, they hadn't noticed John come in.

"Think you've surprised us all except Maria. She sends her best wishes and is looking forward to celebrate tonight."

He went straight to Ben and gave his little brother a big man hug, then he turned to Emma and did the same.

"Welcome to the family, sis," he laughed. The phone went and Bill answered it. It was Mrs. Anderson who wanted to invite everybody round for a barbecue celebration the following evening.

"One moment. I'll have to ask everyone. In the meantime, do you wanna speak to Emma and Ben?"

He called them over. "Emma, it's your mom on the phone."

Whilst they were talking, Bill relayed the message from Mrs. Anderson to the others. They didn't need long to answer yes.

"Tell them it's a yes from us all here," John had popped his head around the corner to make sure Emma had got the message.

After some rather difficult and at times very stressful weeks, it all turned out to be a perfect ending.

That evening, all six of them went off to the local rodeo show and had a wonderful time. What a way to end months of troubles. They could put it all behind them now and start a new chapter.

TBC

Lightning Source UK Ltd.
Milton Keynes UK
UKHW042329020222
398095UK00003B/66